BEWARE!!
DO NOT READ THE
BOOK FROM
BEGINNING TO END!

Guess what's in *store* for you? A midnight treasure hunt in Mayfield's Bazaar! Collect everything on the list, and you and your pal Julie can pick a prize from the store! But don't take a wrong step. Because after twelve, the store comes *alive* . . .

Still want to shop? Look out for the evil watchman. His eyesight is really sharp — and so are his teeth. The mannequins aren't dummies. And they hate kids who take stuff from their store. Oh, and the gargoyles on the roof? They like to party when the moon rises . . . and you're invited.

You're in control of this scary adventure. So beware. You don't want to shop till you drop . . . dead! Start on PAGE 1. Then follow the instructions at the bottom of each page. And *GIVE YOURSELF GOOSEBUMPS!*

READER BEWARE —
YOU CHOOSE THE SCARE!

Look for more
GIVE YOURSELF GOOSEBUMPS adventures
from R.L. STINE

R.L. STINE

GIVE YOURSELF

Goosebumps®

SHOP TILL YOU
DROP . . . DEAD!

AN
APPLE
PAPERBACK

SCHOLASTIC INC.
New York Toronto London Auckland Sydney

A PARACHUTE PRESS BOOK

No part of this publication may be reproduced in whole or in part, or stored in a retrieval system, or transmitted in any form or by any means, electronic, mechanical, photocopying, recording, or otherwise, without written permission of the publisher. For information regarding permission, write to Scholastic Inc., Attention: Permissions Department, 555 Broadway, New York, NY 10012.

ISBN 0-590-39776-1

Copyright © 1998 by Parachute Press, Inc. All rights reserved. Published by Scholastic Inc. APPLE PAPERBACKS and logo are trademarks and/or registered trademarks of Scholastic Inc. GOOSEBUMPS is a registered trademark of Parachute Press, Inc.

12 11 10 9 8 7 6 5 4 3 2 1   8 9/9 0 1 2 3/0

Printed in the U.S.A.   40

First Scholastic printing, January 1998

"Your father's store is *not* cursed," you tell Reggie Mayfield. "And we're going to prove it!"

"Yeah," your best friend, Julie, agrees. "This bet is a cinch."

It's late at night, almost twelve. You, Reggie, and Julie sneaked out of your houses to meet at Mayfield's Bazaar.

You and Julie have a bet with Reggie — and you know you're going to win! All you have to do is spend one hour in the store. One hour after midnight, that is.

If you win, you get to pick anything you want from the store — for free! If you lose, you have to do Reggie's stinking math homework for a month.

"I'm warning you two, you're going to lose!" Reggie insists. "Terrifying things happen in there after midnight. You won't last ten minutes."

"Give me a break, Reggie," you scoff. "We're sick of your stories about how the store is built on cursed ground. And how monsters come out after midnight. We don't believe any of it."

"Yeah! A haunted department store! Puh-leese!" Julie rolls her eyes. "I can't wait to pick —"

Julie suddenly stops talking. Her brown eyes open wide. Her face grows pale as she points a shaking finger at the dark, empty store.

Turn to PAGE 2.

You look where she's pointing. Something is moving in one of the windows of the Bazaar! Something white.

A chill creeps over your skin. Is it . . . a *skeleton*?

You see a flash of red. It's looking your way! With its piercing red eyes!

You're about to scream, when the skeleton blinks. And blinks again. And again. Its eyes look exactly like a car's blinking taillights.

Oh.

Its eyes *are* a car's blinking taillights, reflected in the window. And the skeleton's "body" is a white curtain behind the glass.

Julie must have thought it was a monster too. She's acting really nervous all of a sudden.

"We can still back out," she whispers.

You glance around. The streets are deserted this late at night. Fallen leaves tumble along the pavement, pushed by a cold wind.

You gaze back at the store, with its dark windows and creepy stone carvings and pillars. It looks eerie in the light of the full moon. Maybe the stories are true.

Turn to PAGE 3.

Then you get a grip on yourself. The store isn't cursed!

"Don't worry," you reassure Julie. "Those are just stories. And there are two of us. Besides," you add with a grin, "think of the prize. I'm going to pick a stereo or some Rollerblades!"

"Yeah! I want a snowboard!" Julie nods so hard, her dark curls bounce. "Let's go."

"You'll be sorry," Reggie warns you, shaking his head. "I left you instructions inside."

You and Julie climb the marble stairs to the front door. Julie unlocks it and pushes the door open.

Stay calm, you order yourself, as you peer into the shadows.

You step into the store. Glass cases line the aisles. Dim lights shine on their contents: jewelry, sunglasses, watches.

"Cool!" Julie dashes over to one of the cases. "Splotch watches! I'll borrow one and put it back before we go."

"Good idea," you reply. "That way we'll be sure to get out of here in exactly one hour."

You spot a cardboard sign taped to another case.

"This must be from Reggie!" you call, pointing to it.

Turn to PAGE 4 to read the sign.

4

Julie buckles the Splotch watch onto her wrist and walks over. You both stand there, reading the sign. It says:

"Is that a one or a seven?" you ask Julie.

"I can't tell. Reggie sure has lousy handwriting!" Julie grumbles. "Isn't the floor we're on now Floor One?"

"No, this is the main floor," you tell her.

"Well, do you want to try the first floor or the seventh?" She gazes at you, waiting for an answer.

To explore Floor Seven, turn to PAGE 60.
To check out Floor One, turn to PAGE 9.

You're scared. What if you rub the ape the wrong way?

But you take a deep breath and tickle his chest. The ape grunts. You scratch his back. The ape closes his eyes and huffs.

"Put me down now," you order. He blinks and sets you gently to the ground. "He understands!" you exclaim. "And he likes me."

The ape kisses you on the forehead.

"Let's show Reggie," Julie suggests.

"Carry us downstairs," you order the ape.

It lifts you and Julie in its burly arms and trots downstairs and out of the store. It sets you down in front of an astonished Reggie.

"Th-that looks like Bingo," Reggie stammers. He points at the ape. "He's a stuffed animal on display on the seventh floor."

"He came to life at midnight," you say.

"We won the bet," Julie declares. "We got everything you put on the list." She dumps out the duffel bag in front of Reggie.

"I guess you two are braver than I thought." Reggie sighs. "A bet is a bet. You get to pick whatever you want from the store."

You know what you're going to pick. . . .

It's stuffed during the day, but at night it eats bananas, and it can give you a lift to anywhere . . . swinging on a vine!

THE END

ZIP! ZAM! Arrows fly at you and Julie!

"Take cover!" you shout. You drag Julie behind a big pyramid of basketballs.

BANG! BANG! Arrows pierce the basketballs, popping them.

"Who's shooting at us?" Julie's voice trembles with fear.

Your heart pounds. You peek around the balls.

You spot the shooter. He's an old-fashioned archer wearing a vest and leggings. On his head sits a pointed hat with a long curved feather on it.

BAM! BANG! Two more basketballs pop. Your heart jumps.

"He looks crazy!" you tell Julie. "What should we do?"

"I can think of two things," she answers. "We could hold up a white flag and call a truce. Or we could try to bean him in the head with these basketballs."

"He'll probably shoot us if we try to surrender," you mutter. "Then again, I never heard of using basketballs as weapons."

"Well, I don't hear *you* coming up with any great plans. We have to do something," Julie whispers.

To surrender, flip to PAGE 107.

To hit the archer with basketballs, dribble to PAGE 16.

"We should use the ladder," you decide. "Sliding down the cable is too dangerous."

The building shimmies and shakes as you and Julie crouch at the edge of the elevator shaft.

Julie grabs the top rung of the ladder. She stretches out a foot and carefully sets it in place. Then she swings her other leg over. "It's not too slippery," she tells you.

She disappears down the shaft. You ease onto the ladder and start down after her.

"Oh, no!" Julie cries from below.

"What is it?" you call.

"The ladder . . . it disappears!"

"What do you mean, it disappears?" you demand. You cling to the ladder in the dark elevator shaft.

"It just stops!" Julie shouts.

Hang on until PAGE 118.

"Sorry," you tell the gargoyles. "But we don't want to take the test. We brought climbing gear up here. And if it's okay with you, we'll just climb down to the street. Right, Julie?"

"Right!" Julie chimes in quickly. She doesn't seem to want to take the test, either.

"I'm afraid you're out of luck," Craig T. Kelly replies, shaking his head sadly. "Brueckner, tell them what you did."

A gargoyle steps forward, hanging his head down in shame. He is tall and thin, except for a bulging belly. His arms hang down to the ground, claws grating on the roof.

"I ate all your equipment," the gargoyle named Brueckner confesses. "That rope sure was tasty."

Without a rope, you have no chance of getting down. And since you're not willing to take the test, you just have to stay with the gargoyles forever. They won't let you go.

After a while, you get used to perching on the ledge during the day and roaming the roof at night.

There's only one real downside. The pigeons. They keep dropping little "presents" on you.

SPLAT!

THE END

"We might as well start on the first floor," you tell Julie. "It's the closest one."

"Sounds good to me." Julie points to a large, old-fashioned elevator with polished brass doors. "Let's take the elevator."

As the doors slide open, you spot a big, brand-new duffel bag in the elevator car. Then you notice a piece of lined notebook paper taped to the wood-paneled wall.

Read it on PAGE 122.

"*GONG!*" A clock strikes one. Clocks all over the store chime. Reggie moans and stumbles backwards.

"It's one o'clock!" you cry. "The midnight hour is over!"

"We did it!" Julie exclaims.

The backpack releases your hands. It falls to the ground.

"Reggie's turning back into a kid again!" Julie points at the terrifying giant.

Your eyes widen as you watch Reggie shrink to normal size. His skin changes color.

"What happened?" Reggie asks. He seems sleepy.

"We won the bet! That's what happened!" Julie announces triumphantly.

Reggie smiles broadly. "I tell you what . . . why don't we go double or nothing. What are you guys doing tomorrow around midnight?"

THE END
(right?)

BAM! POP! Perfume bottles start exploding all around the room. You've got to get to the elevators — fast!

But how? You can't see a thing.

And the smell. It's so sickeningly sweet. You feel as if you might faint.

You drop to your knees and start crawling. When you reach a wall, you stand up and grope around with your hands. You feel a switch for a fire alarm. It gives you an idea.

If you pull the alarm, the sprinklers will come on. That would clear the perfume out of the air so you could see your way to the elevator!

But it might also alert the fire department. Then you'd be in even bigger trouble.

Maybe I should just use the wall as a guide to feel my way to the elevator, you think.

BANG! ZAP!

More bottles are breaking.

Do something! Quick!

To pull the fire alarm, go to PAGE 119.
To feel your way to the elevator, go to PAGE 83.

Where is luck when you need it?

Not on the third floor with you, Julie, and the Heart Attack Backpack.

"I can't find anything sharp on this whole floor!" Julie shouts to you. "Maybe there's time for me to go to another . . ." Her voice trails off as she stares at you.

You look back weakly. Your heart feels as if it has burst — and now is too weak to beat. Your body goes limp. The backpack releases your neck and shoulders. It hops onto your belly.

As your vision grows dim, you can just make out Julie. She stumbles over to you. She stares at the backpack.

Julie's eyes are glazed.

Oh, no! you realize. She's under the spell of the Heart Attack Backpack.

It must be calling to her, just as it did to you.

You wish you could help her, but your heart is about to give out.

You know what Julie's thinking: Wear the backpack, the backpack is my friend, the backpack loves me.

Too bad for Julie — that backpack is a real heartbreaker!

THE END

"This is a perfect setup to trip the vampire," you tell Julie. "Let's go for it."

You remember that you have a yo-yo in the pocket of your jacket. You and Julie quickly stretch the string across the top step, at ankle level.

The door bursts open, and the vampire charges through. His eyes burn with furious red fire. He doesn't notice the string.

TWANG! The string trips him! The vampire goes flying down the slippery stairs. *THUMP, THUMP, THUMP.* He lands on the floor below. He lies motionless.

"We did it!" Julie shouts. Her voice echoes down the stairway.

You gaze down at the vampire. He looks as if he's unconscious. But he might just be pretending. You and Julie shouldn't try to get past him, you realize.

"We've got to find some other way of getting out of here," you tell Julie.

Turn to PAGE 15.

"Get it off me!" you pant to Julie. "Pry it off with one of those bats!"

As Julie runs for a bat, you hear a zipping noise.

OW! Something is tugging your hair. You glance over your shoulder.

You can't believe it.

The zipper to the main compartment is open. And the backpack is crunching on your hair!

It burps.

The sides of the compartment smack together. Like lips.

Then the mouth of the backpack widens.

You strain away from the zipper teeth. But the backpack tightens its hold. Its mouth gapes open. And swallows your head!

Looks like you've lost your battle with the backpack.

But the backpack is happy. In the short time it spent with you, it definitely got ahead!

THE END

How are we going to get out of this store? you ask yourself. You can tell Julie is thinking the same thing.

As you stand together in the stairway, gazing down at the vampire, the building begins to tremble again.

"Oh, no!" Julie cries. "It must be some sort of aftershock!"

"We've got to get out of here now!" you declare. You glance at the yo-yo in your hands. It gives you an idea.

"Hey! If we could find some rope, we could climb down the outside of the building," you suggest.

The floor shakes under your feet. You grab on to the railing to keep your balance. "I learned how to climb down a cliff at camp this summer. It's called rappelling. It's easy!"

"Great idea," Julie yells over the rumbling. "Sporting goods is on this floor! We ran right through it."

Get yourself to sporting goods on PAGE 76.

"Let's knock his block off with the basketballs," you declare.

Julie nods.

You grab a ball and start to stand up. A hand wraps around your neck.

Yikes!

The evil archer has each of you by the back of the neck. While you and Julie were plotting, he sneaked around behind you.

"Planning to steal my arrows, were you?" he booms.

"No, we were just . . . ," you begin.

"Silence!" the archer commands. He releases his tight hold on you and Julie. "Now run!"

Huh? He's letting you go?

One glance at his mean face and you figure you'll just keep that question to yourself.

You and Julie start to race for the elevator. An arrow flies by your left ear! Then another zings over Julie's shoulder.

Now you understand. The archer is tired of his usual targets. He wants some *moving* targets.

You should take the advice of those little plastic birds from the shooting gallery:

DUCK!

THE END

GONG! GONG! GONG! The final strokes ring out.

"Midnight. Time for the bet to start," you announce.

As you and Julie get up, you feel a strange rumble.

A tremendous jolt shakes the floor! You fall to your knees. Julie lands on her back.

"What is going on?" she cries.

What *is* going on? you wonder. Then you remember Reggie's stories about how earthquakes shake the store at midnight.

"Earthquake!" you scream.

The carpeted floorboards shriek and twist. With great groaning sounds, they pull apart.

The floor is collapsing!

"Forget the bet!" you shout to Julie. "We've got to get out of here!"

A huge hunk of plaster falls from the ceiling. It lands three inches from Julie's head!

"The stairs!" you scream. "WHERE ARE THE STAIRS?"

Race to PAGE 82.

You frantically rifle through the duffel bag as Reggie gropes his way toward you. Your hand lands on what you want: the battered mannequin's leg.

"Let's trip him with this!" You show Julie the leg.

"Perfect," Julie replies.

You stick the leg out in front of the mutant's path.

WHAM! Reggie trips over it. "Whoooooaaah!" he bellows.

CRAAASSHHH! He lands on a china display.

The mutant moans and rubs his head. He struggles to sit up in the mountain of crushed teacups and plates.

"Nice shot!" Julie laughs.

At the sound of Julie's laughter, Reggie growls with anger. Before you can move, he jumps to his feet and grabs Julie!

The gigantic monster-boy raises Julie over his head. It looks like he's going to smash her to the ground.

"Help!" she shrieks.

Do something!

If you have the scroll from the archer, use its charms on PAGE 106.

If you don't have the scroll, try to use the mannequin's leg to make Reggie drop Julie on PAGE 129.

"Let's smush the termites," you call to Julie. "Roll around!"

"Okay," Julie replies. You both thrash back and forth. The little bug bodies squish and pop.

It works! You smush all the termites.

"We did it!" you declare. You try to sit up.

You can't.

You pull and struggle.

But the goo from the termite bodies is hardening around you. It's turning rock solid. And you're trapped.

Like a bug in a rug.

A termite rug!

THE END

You'll feed the mech-animals. Then, when they're distracted, you'll escape!

You fumble for the bag of peanuts in your pocket. Ripping the cellophane open, you sprinkle the peanuts on the ground.

"Come and get it!" you cry.

"NO!" Dr. Mayfield screams. "They can't eat! NO!"

You ignore the scientist. "Come on, critters." The animals gobble up the peanuts you have spread on the floor.

"You fool!" Dr. Mayfield shouts. "They aren't designed to eat regular food. They'll go haywire."

Uh-oh. You glance down at the mech-animals around your feet.

Turn to PAGE 127.

The judge and jury are waiting for your plea.

"Well, you didn't mean to do it," you whisper to Julie. "But you *did* leave the store with the watch . . . so let's plead guilty. Maybe they will go easy on us."

Julie nods. "Your honor, we plead guilty," she declares.

"Very well," the judge booms. "Jury, what is your sentence?"

A mannequin rises stiffly to her feet. "We sentence the defendants to — total banishment!"

The courtroom erupts in shouting.

"They're just kids!" calls one mannequin.

"Too cruel," another yells.

"Order! ORDER!" The judge pounds his gavel. "The sentence begins now. Escort these defendants out of the store — *forever*!"

You and Julie are seized by the policeman mannequin and hauled out of the store.

"You two are banished!" he barks at you. "Never come back." He walks back into the store.

You burst out laughing. "That's it? We get thrown out?"

"The mannequins must love the store so much that this is the worst thing they can imagine," Julie replies with a grin.

"Well, I never want to step foot in that place again!" you announce. "So I would say this is one happy

END."

"Poisonous Perfume doesn't sound too hard," Julie suggests. "Let's go get that."

You press the button for Floor Two. "You don't think it's really poison, do you?"

Julie laughs. "Maybe Reggie just thinks all perfume smells like poison."

The elevator lurches into motion and then clunks to a halt. As the doors slide open, you and Julie prepare yourselves for an attack. But everything seems quiet and still.

"Over there," Julie whispers. She points to a glass table covered with perfume bottles in different shapes and sizes.

"Look at them all!" you exclaim. "How are we going to find the bottle on Reggie's list?"

"Let's just grab one and go," Julie replies. "All we have to do is prove we've been here."

"But maybe one of the perfumes is *called* Poisonous Perfume!" you argue. "If we don't give Reggie that one, we'll lose the bet!"

"If we don't hurry up, we're going to lose the bet anyway," Julie retorts, tapping her foot impatiently.

You stare at the hundreds of bottles, wondering what to do.

To look for Poisonous Perfume, turn to PAGE 71.

To grab any bottle and keep going, turn to PAGE 26.

The monkey scurries back up the pulley. It climbs about three feet, then hops into a square opening in the wall of the elevator shaft. You didn't notice it before. It looks like some kind of ventilation shaft. It could be a tunnel!

"I think there's a way out!" you exclaim.

With a heave, you pull yourself into the opening. You lie flat and slip down a slick passageway, gaining speed as you go. You hear Julie scramble in after you.

WHOOSH! You fly out of the chute. *THUMP!* You land on a big soft cushion.

"Finally! You're here," comes a voice from a dark corner.

Who said that? You gaze around.

A small table lamp casts a dim light. From what you can see, you are in a big cement room stocked with weird scientific equipment.

Julie lands on the cushion behind you. The little monkey tumbles out with a clatter.

"I've been waiting for you," the voice declares.

Waiting? For you? Why?

Find out on PAGE 68.

You gaze lovingly at the glowing green backpack. You run your hands over its cool plastic mesh. You pick it up and slip it onto your back.

Ahhhhhh!

It fits snugly. You can feel the glow through your sweater.

Thump, *thump*. Thump, *thump*.

Julie rushes up to you. "Why are you grinning like an idiot?" she asks. She snaps her fingers in your face.

"HELLO?!" she shouts. "Can you hear me? Snap out of it!"

You ignore Julie. You are in a happy daze. You love the backpack . . . and the backpack loves you!

The backpack is hugging you.

It's hugging you very hard.

Actually, it's *squeezing* you.

Tight! Tighter! *Tighter*.

Ack! You can't breathe!

Turn to PAGE 73. Before it's too late!

You decide that your best bet is to get away from the gargoyles. With their twisted faces and spiky teeth they look dangerous.

"Julie," you whisper, handing her a climbing harness. "Put this on. Distract them while I set up the rope. Then we'll rappel down together. Okay?"

Julie nods solemnly. She quickly pulls on her harness.

"Hey, look at me!" she yells, darting away from you. "Catch me if you can, you freaks!"

The gargoyles hoot and growl. All twelve of them follow Julie. You quickly tie the rope to one of the giant smokestacks and slip into your mountain-climbing harness.

"Hey! Over here, you weird wall ornaments!" you shout. The gargoyles all turn around and glare at you.

The gargoyles hobble toward you. Clouds of furious steam puff from their nostrils.

"Later, dudes!" You ease yourself over the edge of the building. You have a good hold on the rope — you're home free!

This is going to be a piece of cake.

Slide down to PAGE 84.

"You're right, Julie," you agree. "Any one of these bottles will do just fine." You snatch a tall, skinny bottle of golden-colored perfume from the table.

"I want to check out the sixth floor," Julie calls over her shoulder as she heads back toward the elevator. "We're supposed to find volcano steam. That sounds really cool."

"That does sound cooooooooo — !" Your words turn into a shriek as you stumble and fall. The rug moved under your feet!

"Whoa!" Julie cries as she falls too.

You can feel the rug squirming as you lie on it, dazed.

"What the . . . ?" you mutter. You clamber to your feet and yank back the rug.

"Bugs!" Julie exclaims. "Yuck!"

Gross! A gazillion white slimy termites squirm on the floor.

Turn to PAGE 74.

"We don't have anything that gives off light!" you whisper. "We have to find a light switch."

SNORT! GRUNT!

The thing is coming closer!

"Let's split up and try to find one on the wall," you suggest.

You and Julie stumble away from each other in the dark.

"Ow," you yelp. You rub your shin. "Must have banged into a table," you mutter.

Finally, your outstretched hands brush against something smooth. The wall! Good, now you can search for a light switch.

You run your hands along the slick surface of the painted wall. The texture changes. You're running your hands along something furry.

Gross! It almost feels like some kind of animal.

Uh-oh. *Are* you rubbing an animal? And is it . . . friendly?

Find out on PAGE 78.

A pale man turns the corner. He wears an official-looking navy blue uniform. The night watchman! He shines his flashlight on you and Julie. The werewolf growls and bares its hideous yellow teeth.

"Look out, mister!" Julie warns. "There's a werewolf in here!"

The man raises one eyebrow at you and Julie. Then he purses his lips and whistles.

The werewolf instantly becomes calm and relaxed. It pads over to the guard and sits at his feet.

Your mouth drops open in surprise. This guard must have some magical powers. He has a werewolf for a guard dog!

"Thanks for saving us, sir," you say politely. "The building started shaking, and then your dog was in the way of the emergency exit. We'll just be going now." You edge toward the stairs.

"NOT SO FAST!" the guard commands. His eyes burn bloodred. As you stare, he opens his mouth and hisses.

He has two gleaming white fangs and a forked black tongue!

Oh, no! "A vampire!" you shout. "Run!"

Race to PAGE 87.

"There's no way we can hide from that monster," you decide. "We'll have to fight him."

"But how can we with our hands trapped inside this stupid backpack?" Julie demands.

Good question.

Too bad you don't come up with a good answer.

CHOMP!

MUNCH, MUNCH, MUNCH, CRUNCH, MUNCH.

GULP.

Your only consolation is that when Reggie gobbles down you and Julie, you give him an awful stomachache.

So in some small way, you come out winners in

THE END.

"Look how slowly they're moving!" you whisper to Julie. "I'm sure we can outrun them. And we need the leg to win the bet!"

"GIVE US THE LEG!" the mannequins chant. Their plastic fingers stretch toward you.

"Let's run!" Julie yells.

You both burst through the circle of mannequins and race for the elevator. Julie clutches the mannequin's leg.

More dummies are coming. You dodge the slow-moving mannequins. To the left . . . the right . . . you're almost there. . . .

SMACK! You run into the broad plastic chest of a mannequin wearing a ski outfit. He falls on top of you, pinning you to the ground.

"Give me the leg!" the mannequin demands.

You glance over his shoulder. The other mannequins have caught up. Even if you could get free, you wouldn't be able to fight your way past this angry plastic mob.

"Get help!" you beg Julie. "Get my parents! Get the police!"

Julie leaps into the elevator. But it's too late. By the time help arrives, the mannequins have already divided you up for spare parts.

This bet cost you way too much. In fact, it cost you an arm AND A LEG!

THE END

You decide to slide faster. Otherwise your arms may give out. Eight floors is a long way down.

You release your grip slightly. The elevator cable slides more easily through your hands. You pick up speed.

Too much speed.

Your gloves are slick from the grease on the cable. You zoom down

down

down. . . .

Unfortunately you forgot how you got into this situation in the first place. The elevator cables broke — remember?

Including the cable you are zipping down.

Which means there's a three-story drop between the end of the cable and the ground.

Better close the book right now. Really. Not to leave you *dangling*, but you don't want to *hang* around. Because you can't hold on forever. You will finally have to let go in

THE END.

You're in serious trouble — it's time for serious action. You decide to take one of the animals hostage. Maybe you can use it to bargain for your freedom.

You bend over and scoop up a tiny metal kitten. "You let me and my friend go or the kitten gets it!" you announce forcefully.

"Don't hurt Valdez!" Dr. Mayfield exclaims.

Your plan seems to be working! Julie snatches up a mech-dog.

Dr. Mayfield drops to her knees, begging. "Don't hurt my little friends! I'll do anything you say! Creatures — sit!"

The tiny mechanical animals immediately stop their attack.

"Please, put them down," the scientist pleads. "I'll let you go. Or I'll show you my greatest invention! My time machine."

You stare at the scientist. "You have a time machine?" you demand. "And it works?"

Dr. Mayfield nods vigorously. "You can use it!"

A time machine! Awesome! If Dr. Mayfield could make these mutant toys, she probably *could* build a time machine.

"What do you think?" you ask Julie. She shrugs.

It's up to you. Do you want to check out the scientist's time machine? Or do you want her to lead you back to the main floor?

To try the time machine, turn to PAGE 123.
To just get out of there, turn to PAGE 42.

"'Floor Three: Heart Attack Backpack,'" you read from Reggie's note. "What is that?"

"Who knows?" Julie answers. "But I guess we'll find out."

She presses the button. As the elevator moves to the third floor, you put your hand on your heart.

Yep, still beating.

And you hope a Heart Attack Backpack won't do anything to change that!

The elevator doors slide open. Your eyes land on a wall of backpacks. A glowing neon green one hangs in the middle.

You step closer to read its label:

HEART ATTACK BACKPACK

The backpack seems to pulse slowly. Thump, *thump*. Thump, *thump*. Thump, *thump*. Like a heartbeat.

You are suddenly dying to wear the backpack. You can't resist. You reach your hand out.

"Hey!" Julie calls. "Wait up! Hold on!"

But you ignore her. All you care about is the backpack . . . touching the backpack . . . wearing the backpack. . . .

Turn to PAGE 24.

Molten rock tumbles down the volcano's side and bounces toward you. The heat from the volcano burns your face.

"Let's get out of here," you cry. You press the Door Close button on the elevator. The doors slide shut.

You hit the button for the main floor. Nothing happens. Frantically, you press *all* the buttons. Instead of taking you down, the elevator starts shaking. It bounces up and down, side to side. You feel as if your brain is being scrambled!

A hissing sound grows louder and louder. *HISSS!* The sound becomes a high-pitched whistle, like the noise a kettle makes when the water is boiling.

WHEEEEEEEE! Steam pours into the elevator through cracks in the floorboards.

"It's steam from the volcano!" Julie yells. "It's building up underneath us!"

Talk about pressure! Now what? Find out on PAGE 50.

If the parent figures get that glitter on Julie, she'll turn into cardboard too!

The father reaches his stiff arm toward Julie.

You must warn her. You desperately point one arm.

Julie drops her hands from her eyes and glances toward you. She sees your pointing finger and whirls around just in time. She grabs a teddy bear from a display and hurls it at the father.

He topples over!

The cardboard figures are so light that a stuffed animal can knock them down.

Pile stuff on them, Julie! you think.

She must have the same idea. She starts tossing teddy bears and stuffed pigs on the parents. She buries them in plush animals. They can't dig themselves out — they're too light.

"We don't have to worry about them anymore," Julie declares. "But what are we going to do about *you*? You're cardboard!"

Turn to PAGE 96.

You stand in the doorway of the store, frozen with terror!

The werewolf flies toward you . . . and goes right by you! He scrambles down the front steps and races into the woods across the street! He wasn't chasing you at all — he just wanted to get out of the crumbling store as much as you did!

"The werewolf is a chicken!" Julie exclaims.

"I don't blame him," you reply. "I was pretty scared too!"

You scan the street. Reggie is nowhere to be seen! Maybe the werewolf scared him away, you think.

"Let's get out of this place," Julie urges.

"You got it!" you answer. Together, you and Julie step onto the stone steps of the Bazaar.

"*Not so fast*," booms a stern voice, right into your ear.

Two strong hands grab you by the arms and spin you around.

Plastic hands!

You are face-to-face with a plastic dummy — a mannequin! Wearing a policeman's cap!

Turn to PAGE 41.

"Give me the Heart Attack Backpack!" you order Julie. "Maybe it will choke him!"

Julie tries to fish the backpack out of the duffel bag. But she can't seem to get it.

"It grabbed my hands!" she wails. "Help me!"

You dig into the duffel bag. But your hands are gripped by the Heart Attack Backpack. You're stuck — just like Julie.

"What are we going to do?" Julie whimpers.

"I'm getting hungrier!" Reggie screams. He stomps closer.

"Hide!" you shriek. With your hands still stuck in the Heart Attack Backpack, you and Julie manage to stumble out from behind the counter. Together, you scurry behind another display.

"Now what?" Julie whispers.

"We have two choices," you figure. "If we can survive until one in the morning, we're safe. That's when Reggie turns normal."

"That's a big *if*," Julie comments.

"You're not going to like the other choice, either," you warn her. "That's to fight him."

"Great," Julie moans. "You decide. Those choices are awful!"

You heard her — choose!

To hold out until one A.M., *turn to PAGE 97.*
To battle the giant boy, turn to PAGE 29.

"Monster! Where?" you cry.

The wind on the roof raises the hair on the back of your neck. Or maybe it's pure terror.

Your eyes scan the moonlit landscape of the roof. You spot it. Near the edge. A hulking shape with pointed ears. Bony knees poke out at its sides. You can see sharp talons digging into the pedestal the monster is perched on. The beast is very still. . . .

Too still.

"Wait a minute," you mutter. "That's not a monster. That's a gargoyle! It's a statue made out of stone! I've noticed them on the Bazaar during the day. They're just decorations!"

"Are you sure?" Julie asks. Her hands shake as she smooths down her curly hair. "Wow, I feel so dumb!"

"Don't sweat it," you reply. "After what we've seen tonight, I don't blame you."

You walk to the edge of the roof and glance down. Everything on the ground looks so small! You take a deep breath — this is going to be harder than you expected.

You glimpse another stone gargoyle to your left, out of the corner of your eye. You turn your head to look at it.

AND IT TURNS TO LOOK AT YOU!

Race to PAGE 39.

The gargoyle is alive! It grins at you in the moonlight.

Fear flips your stomach over. Your heart thumps double time.

"Julie!" you shout. "The gargoyles! They're alive!"

A movement to your right catches your eye. Oh, no! It's another gargoyle! This one has huge bug eyes and a mouth full of jagged teeth. It rubs its claws together slowly.

You back away from the edge of the building, toward Julie. You shake from head to toe, and it's not from the wind. Julie grips your hand.

"We're surrounded!" she gasps.

Quick, turn to PAGE 98.

"I know!" Julie shouts. She slaps her forehead. "We already have a sharp thing! The silver arrow!" She yanks the arrow out of the duffel bag and races to you.

Julie saws at the straps of the backpack with the arrow tip.

The backpack goes crazy! It thrashes wildly. It drags you across the floor. The straps of the backpack whip around as it throws you from side to side. The plastic buckles smack your face.

And it clings even tighter to you. A tight death grip.

You've got to get it off *now*!

You grab the arrow from Julie. You glance over one shoulder. And plunge the arrow into the center of the backpack.

"Eeeeeeeee!" The backpack emits a sickening, eerie shriek. It gives a final, wild thrash and goes limp. You yank it off and hurl it to the ground.

"You did it!" Julie exclaims. "I didn't stab it because I was afraid I'd hurt you."

You gingerly pick up the lifeless backpack and thrust it into the duffel bag.

"Let's get off this floor!" you pant as you and Julie head for the elevator. "And let's not forget our one-hour deadline!"

Turn to PAGE 99 to pick another floor.

"Get back in here!" the policeman mannequin commands. He drags you and Julie back into the Bazaar.

The building has stopped shaking. But now a red strobe light flashes rhythmically, and an alarm bell is ringing.

"You dirty, rotten shoplifters!" the mannequin accuses you.

You stare at the living dummy. The sight of its motionless features speaking makes your blood run cold.

"Wha-wha-what are you talking about?" you stammer.

"This!" the mannequin exclaims. He grabs Julie's arm and lifts it up. The Splotch watch!

"I forgot to put it back!" Julie gasps. "I was going to!"

"That's what they all say!" the mannequin retorts. "It's not bad enough we had an earthquake, but shoplifting too! It takes a lot of work for us mannequins to run this joint. And kids like you don't appreciate it. You're coming with me."

The mannequin shoves you and Julie down the aisle. You gape at the bizarre sight around you. Now that the earthquake is over, crews of mannequin workers are cleaning up the store and setting everything in order.

"Mannequins run this store?" you whisper to Julie in shock.

Flip to PAGE 75.

"This woman is dangerous," you murmur to Julie. "Let's get as far away from her as we can."

Julie nods. "I'm with you."

"Lead us to the main floor," you demand.

"Hand over my pets and I'll show you the way," the scientist replies.

You hand her the metal kitten. Julie gives her the dog. After making sure they're all right, Dr. Mayfield crosses over to the console and presses a big red button.

You stare, stunned, as part of the concrete wall slides open, revealing a set of wooden stairs.

You and Julie climb the creaky wooden stairs. You push open the door at the top and find yourself back on the main floor.

Amazing. No damage! The fake earthquake had no effect.

"That was so weird." You shudder, watching the door slam shut.

"More like terrifying," Julie replies. "But I still want to try to win the bet."

"Let's start on the first floor this time," you suggest.

You find the elevator. The doors are open, and it looks undamaged. A note is tacked to the wall.

"Look!" you exclaim. "That must be a message for us."

Step into the elevator on PAGE 122.

You stare at Dr. Mayfield, your eyes wide with terror. She's insane! you realize with growing horror. There will be no way to reason with her.

"How will we fight them?" Julie whispers. "I don't even understand what they are!"

You gaze at the mech-animals. They are strange, twisted creatures. Each is made of bits and pieces of real animals — you spot tigers, dogs, cats, birds — and metal junk. Their jaws click on hinges as they bite at the air. Their metal claws grate on the cement floor.

Maybe you can try to win the mechanical creatures over to your side. You remember you have a bag of peanuts in your pocket. If you feed them, they might like you.

Or maybe you could grab one of the animals and take it hostage. That way you could force the scientist to open the door.

To feed the animals, turn to PAGE 20.
To take a hostage, turn to PAGE 32.

"Baby booties?" Julie reads from the list. "That sounds easy! Let's go to Floor Four."

"Gee, I'm pretty scared of baby booties," you joke.

"Oooh, me too," Julie adds, pressing the Floor Four button. "A couple of pairs of baby booties ganged up on me in an alley once! They tickled me pretty bad."

You're both snorting and giggling as the elevator doors open. You step onto the fourth floor.

The baby clothes department is right in front of you. You immediately spot three cardboard figures: a mom, a dad, and a baby. And the baby is wearing little knit slippers! Perfect!

"It's like taking candy from a baby," you say, grinning.

As you lift up the display baby to pluck off the slippers, you notice something strange. It's coated in silver glitter. The glitter sticks to your left arm.

You feel a tingling. The prickling feeling spreads up your arm to your chest.

"Are you okay?" Julie asks with concern. "You look a little pale."

You gasp as your chest tingles. "Something terrible is happening to me!"

Race to PAGE 104.

"It's too dangerous to go down the elevator shaft. We might fall," you call to Julie. You hope she can hear you over the rumble of the trembling building. "If we're going to get out of here, we've got to take the stairs!"

"Then we'd better run!" Julie shouts back.

An elaborate crystal chandelier crashes to the floor inches away. With a burst of energy, you and Julie sprint across the floor, ducking falling plaster and jumping over fallen merchandise. You are only a few feet away from the Exit sign when you skid to a stop.

An animal crouches in front of the door to the stairs!

A furry, four-legged animal.

A big animal.

Make that a *very* big animal.

Turn to PAGE 81.

"No! You got it wrong!" Reggie shouts triumphantly. "There were six volcanoes in the puzzle! Six! Ha-ha-ha!"

"Big deal!" you snap. "So I didn't get it completely right. So what?"

"You don't get any volcano steam!" Reggie quips. "That's what!"

"Too bad for us." Julie rolls her eyes. "We don't get the volcano steam. But we still can pick another floor!"

"Whatever you say," Reggie's voice echoes from the intercom. "Good luck! You'll need it!"

Turn to PAGE 99 to pick another floor.

You exchange nervous glances with Julie. You don't like the hard, tough expression on the gargoyle's face.

"What's the test, Mr. Kelly?" you ask the gargoyle.

"Well, you see, we gargoyles have to protect ourselves. I mean, if anyone knew we were living, breathing creatures, they'd come up here with big nets and try to put us in the zoo," the gargoyle explains. "So you two have to prove that you'll keep quiet!"

"We would never turn you guys in," you promise sincerely.

The gargoyle puffs up his chest and clears his throat.

"In order to prove that you are trustworthy, the two of you must walk around the ledge of the building. If you get the whole way around without making a sound, we will help you to the ground. Because that will mean that you can really keep your mouths shut."

"But what if we fall?" you ask with a gulp.

Turn to PAGE 52.

The archer raises an eyebrow and crosses his arms. He's waiting to hear why you're on his floor.

"It's-it's-it's this b-b-bet we made with Reggie Mayfield," you stammer, your heart thumping. "We have to get one thing from each floor in the store. We need a silver arrow from sporting goods. I know it's dumb, but we want to win."

The archer lets out a howl of laughter.

"How rich!" He chuckles. "When I was a lad, I made similar wagers with my chums. We young scalawags ruled the village!"

"What is he talking about?" Julie whispers to you.

"He's talking about when he was a kid," you explain. You understand the archer because you read a lot of books. You have a good vocabulary.

"I say," the archer exclaims. His expression grows deadly serious. "Does this wager mean you must confront the fierce beast on the seventh floor?"

Fierce beast? A chill runs down your spine.

Turn to PAGE 57 to find out more.

Your heart pounds in terror as the cold night air rushes by you. The street zooms closer, closer, closer . . . *WHOOSH!*

You are swept up by the strong arms of a gargoyle. Craig T. Kelly!

"Good try, kid," Craig congratulates you. "And you never made a peep. Now we can trust you."

As Craig soars back up to the roof, you spot Reggie down in the street. He's still waiting.

Craig sets you gently on the roof.

Julie dashes over to you, flushed with excitement. A gargoyle with a monkey's face trots beside her.

"I did it!" Julie cries. "I made it all the way around!"

"Great!" you cheer. "And now it's time to win the bet!"

You and Julie climb onto the backs of two gargoyles. They swoop down to the ground behind the store.

"Don't tell anyone about us," Craig reminds you, "and we'll take you flying whenever you want."

You and Julie dash to the front of the store to meet Reggie.

You won! Now you get to pick whatever you want from Mayfield's Bazaar for free. And since you kept your promise, the gargoyles keep theirs: You never need to take the elevator at the store again.

THE END

Rumbling sounds fill the elevator. You and Julie drop to the floor and cover your heads. "It's going to blow!" you holler.

WHOOOSH! The steam shoots the elevator up the shaft. You feel like a bullet being shot out of a gun.

CRASH! The elevator rips through the roof of Mayfield's Bazaar.

What a ride! You and Julie are the first kids in space. And you're the first humans to travel there in an elevator. Not to mention the first to use volcano steam as fuel!

You could have made millions if you ever came back to Earth. Unfortunately, the elevator doesn't turn out to be an ideal space vehicle. For starters, it isn't equipped with navigational controls. Or a life-support system.

Oh, well. Looks like all your dreams just went up in smoke. Volcano smoke, that is.

THE END

"Can I just ask you one question?" Julie pipes up. "How did you make the store stop shaking?"

"I did it with science!" Dr. Mayfield declares. "You can do anything with science. See these animals?" She gestures to dozens of mechanical animals scattered around the cement floor.

You stare at the metal animals. At first you thought they were just regular toys. But now that you take a closer look, you realize there is nothing regular about them.

Tufts of real hair sprout from between their mechanical limbs. Some have bodies that seem to be half metal and half flesh.

"Wh-wh-what are they?" you stammer. The strange-looking animals are totally creepy.

"Toys, of course," the scientist replies. "No one else could have made them but me. I fused together real animal tissue and pieces of scrap metal. They will be the next big toy craze."

Your mouth drops open. She used REAL animals! you realize with a shock. How horrible!

"But I'm wasting my talents on toys," Dr. Mayfield complains. She turns toward you and Julie.

"YOU will be my greatest experiment!" she exclaims.

Yikes! Get over to PAGE 88. Quick!

52

"Enough talk!" a gargoyle shouts. "Time for action."

No one answers your question.

"Are you ready for the test?" Craig T. Kelly demands.

You peer over the edge of the roof. The ledge is about a foot and a half wide. It looks very dangerous.

Maybe you should pass on taking the test and climb down your own way. The gargoyles would let you do that . . . wouldn't they?

To take the test, turn to PAGE 80.

To talk your way out of it and climb down, turn to PAGE 8.

You run over to Julie, and the two of you huddle together, clutching the leg. Your body trembles as the tall mannequins lurch closer.

"I think they're mad at us," Julie squeaks.

The mannequins stride closer and closer. Their plastic eyes glare at you. Soon you'll be surrounded!

"Let's make a run for the elevator," Julie whispers.

"Okay," you reply. "Or we could give them back the leg. Maybe they would let us go."

"I'll do whatever you want," Julie decides. "But whatever we do, let's hurry!"

"Give us the leg," one of them shrieks.

They begin chanting.

"GIVE US THE LEG!" They step closer.

"GIVE US THE LEG!" They reach toward you.

Hands come at you from every direction.

Quick, decide! Do you want to give them the leg, or do you want to make a run for it?

Give them the leg on PAGE 116.
Or shake a leg over to PAGE 30.

54

The werewolf snaps at your heels!

You pump your arms to pick up speed. "We're almost there!" you tell Julie. She nods as she jogs beside you.

You pass a sign that reads: FLOOR 1.

The building rumbles and quakes. You are thrown forward. You stumble down five stairs, crashing onto the landing.

You catch a glimpse of the werewolf, darting down the stairway above you. His eyes flare with red fire.

"This is it!" Julie shouts. "The main floor! We made it!"

You push open the door and race though the maze of crushed glass cabinets. Mannequins lie scattered like wounded soldiers.

"Grrrrrrahh!" The werewolf draws closer behind you. You can hear his claws rip into the Bazaar's plush carpeting.

Together, you and Julie push open the heavy, wooden doors.

You hear a growl right at your back. You whirl around.

The werewolf leaps, his claws reaching for your eyes!

Race to PAGE 36.

"Let's try Floor Five — sporting goods," Julie suggests. "It shouldn't take us long since I know my way around that floor. I was just there with my mom last week to pick out new cleats for soccer."

"Did you notice any silver arrows?" you ask her. "Because that's what we need to get."

"I remember an archery display," Julie replies. The elevator doors slide open on the fifth floor. "Follow me."

You follow Julie past a rack of basketballs. Past some hockey sticks. Past some jump ropes. Finally you see it.

A big stand filled with all kinds of bows and arrows. There are even some leather quivers to hold the arrows.

The hairs on your arms prick up all of a sudden. Your stomach feels jittery. You're being watched — you just know it.

"Let's find a silver arrow and get out of here," you whisper.

ZAM! A glistening arrow zips right by your head and thunks into the wall.

Someone is shooting at you!

Race to PAGE 6.

Your body flutters straight at the whirring, slicing blades of the ceiling fan.

Your body flips around against your will. You see Julie kneeling below, next to the fan she has aimed at you. Her mouth hangs open in shock.

You see Julie's eyes land on the ceiling fan. *Yes!* you think. Now she'll shut off the fan on the ground.

Or maybe not.

"The button is stuck!" she shrieks up to you.

Your flat body whirls toward the blades.

You flip and flap in the wind from the two fans. In fact, the wind is so strong that every speck of glitter blows off your arm!

With a flush of heat, you feel your body burst back to normal.

You're a regular kid again!

You're also as *heavy* as a regular kid again.

"Noooo!" you cry.

You plummet to the ground!

Tumble to PAGE 113.

"We do have to go to Floor Seven," you tell the archer. "It's called the Final Showdown in our instructions. Is there some kind of beast up there?" You try to keep your voice calm, but it quavers.

"Oh, my dear friends, you shall face the scourge of mankind on the seventh floor. But if you are strong and wise, you will emerge victorious. Perhaps."

"Huh?" Julie asks.

"He says we'll beat the monster on the seventh floor," you translate for her. "Maybe."

"Allow me to aid you in a small way," the archer offers. "Take this silver arrow and this magic chant. You will need them." The archer hands Julie an arrow and an ancient-looking scroll. Julie stows them in the duffel bag.

"Sir, we cannot thank you enough!" You bow. It seems like the right thing to do.

"Um, yeah," Julie adds. "Thanks a lot, sir."

"Farewell, young adventurers," the archer shouts. Then he disappears behind a rack of ice skates.

You and Julie step back into the elevator to pick another floor.

Return to PAGE 99 and choose again.

58

The doors open onto the seventh floor. The first thing you see is . . . nothing.

The entire floor is pitch-black.

"Grab on to my jacket," you tell Julie. "We don't want to get separated." Cautiously, you both step into the darkness.

You stop short. You cock your head. You hear something! And there's no mistaking that sound.

Deep, hoarse breathing. Right ahead of you.

The breaths come in heavy, coarse grunts. And they're growing louder. Closer.

"There's something up here with us," you whisper. "We've got to find a light switch. Fast!"

"Wait." Julie tugs your sleeve. "Do we have something in the duffel bag that shines a light?"

CRASH! Whatever it is just knocked something over.

Whatever it is sounds big.

Whatever it is, is coming for *you*.

Volcano steam gives off light! If you have a jar of it, use it on PAGE 79.

If you don't have any volcano steam, don't freak out. Just go find a light switch on PAGE 27.

"Come out, come out wherever you are!" the vampire guard calls.

SNIFF! SNIFF! The werewolf tries to track your scent.

"Julie," you whisper. You point to the hole and a nearby rack of coats. "Push the rack over the hole. Then use the coats to cover the hole in the floor. I'll distract the guard."

Julie sneaks out of her hiding place. Crawling on her hands and knees, she crosses to the coats. When you see she is in position to push over the rack, you stand up.

"Catch me if you can!" you shout at the guard and the werewolf.

They dash toward you. The vampire grins, and his fangs gleam. You dart around the floor, jumping over toppled mannequins and dodging behind glass cases.

You head for the fallen rack of coats, but as you draw near it . . . you trip. You go sprawling.

Right behind you, the werewolf lets out a blood-curdling howl of delight as you slide across the floor.

Race to PAGE 115.

"Let's start at the top and work our way down," you suggest.

"Floor Seven it is!" Julie agrees. "There's the elevator."

The two of you stroll across the dimly lit showroom. Julie steps up to the elevator and presses the button. The antique brass doors slide open and you walk in.

"It's two minutes before midnight," Julie announces, checking her borrowed Splotch watch. "We can explore this whole store in a half hour, easy."

"We are totally going to win this bet!" You grin.

The elevator glides up and opens onto the seventh floor. You stand there, gazing out.

Everything is still. Dim security lights shine down on stacks of neatly folded women's sweaters. Racks of dresses line the walls. "Seems okay," you declare.

SNAP! You hear a sound at the top of the elevator. You grab the wall to keep your balance as the elevator lurches. *POP! PING!*

It sounds as if the cables holding the elevator are breaking!

The elevator doors start to close. Trapping you inside!

"Quick!" you shout. "Jump out!"

Leap to PAGE 72.

You burrow deeper into the socks. You hope the vampire night guard and his werewolf guard dog don't discover your hiding place.

You squeeze your eyes shut. You can hear the werewolf slobbering around the bin.

CRASH. You tumble out of the bin in a shower of socks. The werewolf knocked over the bin. You forgot that werewolves have a very powerful sense of smell. The beast tracked you right to your hiding place.

"Aaaahh!" you scream, more in fear than in pain, when the werewolf sinks its teeth into your arm. Julie pops her head out from behind the clothing rack.

She's really sad when you transform into a werewolf. But not nearly as sad as when you bite her — and she turns into a werewolf too.

Luckily, she'll have all of eternity to forgive you. Because that's how long you'll have guard dog duty together.

THE END

"'Chesh que chesh que looka looka looka!'" you shout, reciting the charm from the scroll.

The giant mutant loses his grip on Julie. She tumbles to the ground. She jumps up, unharmed, and joins you.

"The charm is working!" Julie exclaims.

A powdery orange steam rises from the mutant's skin.

"He's shrinking," you gasp. You watch in awe as a glowing cloud of orange-and-white smoke surrounds Reggie completely.

A minute later, out from the cloud of smoke steps the normal, regular Reggie. He's kid-sized again.

"You saved me!" Reggie dashes over to you and Julie. He throws his arms around you both. "You did it! You broke the curse of the Mayfields! Thank you, thank you!"

When Reggie's dad finds out that you and Julie broke the curse on his department store, he is really grateful. So grateful, in fact, that he lets you go on a major shopping spree!

Your fortune: Good things are in STORE for you!

THE END

You rip the shiny silver cap off the bottle of Poisonous Perfume and aim the nozzle at Reggie's face.

The perfume squirts out in a golden cloud. Reggie screws up his face in pain.

"NGHAAAAAAHHH!" he bellows. You can see his swollen black tongue thrashing in his mouth. He stumbles toward you, groping with his hands.

"He can't see where he's going," Julie whispers. "Let's trip him."

"Great idea!" you reply. You rummage in the duffel bag. "What should we use?"

Stick the mannequin's leg in front of Reggie on PAGE 18.

Stretch the yarn from the baby booties across his path on PAGE 114.

"Wet paper towel?" Julie asks.

You flap your flat head.

"I know!" Julie cries. "I have a better idea than the paper towel. Come with me!"

Julie lifts you up, being careful not to get any glitter on herself. She carries you to the water fountain near the bathroom.

"I'll just rinse off your arm right here!"

Wait a second, you think. You're cardboard. That much water will turn you into mush!

You frantically shake your head, but Julie doesn't notice as she pushes the button. Water gushes up onto you.

By the time Julie realizes what she's done, it's too late. You're pulp!

At least Julie cares about the planet. She recycles you. Hey, better luck the second time around!

THE END

"Go left!" you yell. You dart to the left of the vampire night guard. You skid as you come up to the mannequin. It blocks your way! You can't get past it.

You step up onto the mannequin's platform. You try to squeeze behind it.

A strong hand clamps down on your shoulder. A plastic hand!

"Over here!" the mannequin calls. With the other hand, it grabs Julie.

"Are you after these intruders?" the mannequin asks the vampire.

"Thanks, man." The vampire security officer approaches the mannequin stand. "I'll see that you get a special commendation."

"One more and I'll make Mannequin of the Month for sure," the plastic dummy gushes. He grips you harder.

A broad smile spreads across the vampire's pale face. His fire-red eyes gleam. He opens his mouth, revealing his razor-sharp fangs. He bends toward your neck.

You squeeze your eyes tight. You can't watch. But you can feel the fangs pierce your skin. You know what they say about people who take risks: They're "sticking their neck out."

Well, you just did. And look what happened!

THE END

"Hey, I just made a volcano model for school," Julie tells you. "Let's go to Floor Six. I want to see how theirs looks."

You press Six. The elevator groans into action. *CHUG! CHUG! CREAK!* The elevator starts making noise as it carries you and Julie up.

"I don't like the way that sounds," you comment.

CLANG! SCREECH! With a lurch, the elevator grinds to a halt.

"We're stuck!" Julie bursts out.

The lights go out. It's pitch-black in the elevator.

Then you hear a ghostly chuckle.

"Julie? Is that you?" you ask nervously.

"N-n-n-no," Julie stammers.

"Tee-hee!" The eerie chuckling surrounds you.

Turn to PAGE 93.

The termites squirm over your body, biting you everywhere. Their bodies are slimy and wet. You can hear the sound of hundreds of tiny mouths chewing.

"Spray them!" Julie calls desperately. "Spray them with the perfume."

Perfume? you think. Will that work? Maybe you should roll around and try to smush them all.

CHOMP! CHOMP! The bites prick your skin.

Quick, decide. Before you end up as a midnight snack!

To spray the termites, turn to PAGE 125.
To smush them, turn to PAGE 19.

68

"We've got to get out of here," you warn the hidden person. "The building is falling apart! It's about to collapse!"

"I can take care of that," the voice announces. All the lights burst on. A tall, bony woman wearing a white lab coat sits in front of a panel. It's covered with flashing lights and buttons. The woman presses one of the buttons.

The building stops shaking abruptly.

"My name is Dr. Sheila Mayfield," the woman announces. "My brother owns this store — which you have been sneaking around in. Behave yourselves or I'll turn you in." She glares at you through thick black glasses. Her white hair is piled messily on top of her head.

You gulp. "We'll behave," you promise. "We don't want to make any trouble for anyone. We're just here on a bet —"

"Silence!" she commands.

Turn to PAGE 51.

That werewolf is way too powerful for us to fight, you realize. Better make a run for it.

"GO!" you shout to Julie.

Julie throws the door to the stairway open, and you both race into the stairwell. The door slams shut behind you. You take a moment to lock it. Then you hurtle down the stairs.

CRASH! You hear the sound of the werewolf breaking through the metal door.

"The locked door didn't even slow it down! It's going to get us!" Julie yells.

"Run faster!" you shout back.

SCRITCH! SCRITCH! The sound of the werewolf's nails grinding on the cement floor sends chills up your spine.

You don't even want to think about what will happen if it catches you.

"Faster!" you scream.

The stairs shake under your feet. It feels as if the building will collapse any second!

"Grrahhhh!" The red-eyed werewolf howls behind you.

Speed to PAGE 54.

You show Julie the finished word search. "That's all I can find," you tell her. "Do you see any that I missed?"

Julie studies the puzzle for a minute. "No, I think you got them all," she finally replies.

"Reggie! We're done! Now what?" you call.

"Hold the puzzle up to the security camera in the ceiling. I want to see how many you circled," Reggie instructs you.

You stick the puzzle in front of the glass lens that peers down from the ceiling like a beady eye.

"No!" Reggie's voice booms. "NO! NO! NO!"

"Did I get them all?" you yell. "What's wrong?"

"NOOOOO!" Reggie shouts.

If you found VOLCANO five times or less, go to PAGE 46.

If you found VOLCANO exactly six times, go to PAGE 117.

If you found VOLCANO seven times or more, go to PAGE 85.

"Just give me a minute," you tell Julie. "I'm sure I can find the right bottle."

"Okay," Julie agrees reluctantly. "But remember our one-hour deadline. If you can't find the right bottle soon, just grab any old bottle and let's go!"

"It's a deal," you promise.

You have sixty seconds to find the Poisonous Perfume in the maze above. Time yourself.

If it takes you longer than one minute, go to PAGE 103.

If you find the bottle in time, turn to PAGE 91.

You and Julie dive through the closing doors and roll onto the soft carpet. The elevator doors slam closed behind you.

SNAP! BANG! You hear the rest of the elevator cables tearing. The elevator whooshes down the shaft. *WHAM!* You hear it hit the ground eight stories down.

"That was close," you murmur, feeling stunned.

"I guess we'll be taking the stairs down," Julie jokes shakily.

"Yeah." You lie on the carpet, waiting for your heart to start beating normally again.

GONG! A tremendous ringing sound startles you and Julie.

"What's that?" you gasp. You sit up and glance around.

She points to a large grandfather clock. It lets out a series of *GONG*s. "It's midnight," she whispers. You hear clocks chiming midnight all over the store.

"Well, if Reggie's stories are true, we should see a red-eyed monster any minute," Julie comments.

You know she's joking, but still — you shiver.

Turn to PAGE 17.

The Heart Attack Backpack is squeezing your lungs!

You manage to take a deep breath. Whew! The backpack had you under some kind of spell. But you're okay now.

Is it too late to escape?

"Help me," you croak to Julie.

The backpack grips you tighter and tighter.

Your heart begins to beat faster.

And faster.

AND FASTER!

Thump, *thump*, thump, *thump*, thump, *thump*.

Now you know why it's called a Heart Attack Backpack. You're going to have a heart attack if you don't get it off!

You fumble with the buckles. They're stuck!

Your eyes dart around. You spot a bucket of baseball bats. Julie could try to pry the backpack off with a bat. Or you could try to cut the straps — if you can find something sharp in time.

THUMP, *THUMP*, THUMP, *THUMP*!

Make up your mind. While you still can!

To use the bat, turn to PAGE 14.
To look for something sharp, turn to PAGE 120.

You stare down at the wriggling creatures. There are so many of them, you realize, they made the rug move.

You point at a crack in the floor. "They must be coming from there."

"Well, there aren't any termites on our list, so let's get out of here." Julie steps toward the elevator. But she slips on some termites and lands flat on the floor.

You reach out to help her. But your feet slide on the creepy-crawlers and you flop down beside Julie.

"Gross!" Julie shrieks. "Termites are all over me. Ow! They bite."

The white bugs creep onto your arms and legs. Into your eyes and ears. Every time you try to stand, you slip back down.

"Yeow!" For little critters, they have big bites!

Turn to PAGE 67.

The mannequin policeman marches you to the furniture department.

Twelve mannequins sit in rows of chairs. They're chatting with each other. A robed mannequin wearing a big powdered wig sits on a stand. Another policeman mannequin stands up and announces, "Hear ye, hear ye, let the trial begin."

"We're in a courtroom!" you realize.

The judge glares down sternly at you and Julie.

He points to Julie with a gavel. "You have been caught shoplifting in our store." He gestures toward you. "And you are an accessory to the crime. Everyone knows you did it. Do you plead guilty or not guilty?"

You turn to Julie. There's a desperate look in her eyes.

"Should we plead guilty or not guilty?" you ask her.

"I don't know," she replies. "I don't think we're going to get a fair trial either way. What do you think we should do?"

To plead guilty, turn to PAGE 21.
To plead not guilty, turn to PAGE 121.

You and Julie dash to the sporting goods section.

"This is perfect!" you exclaim, glancing around. "They have everything we need to rappel down the outside of the building."

You sling a coil of rope over your shoulder. You and Julie grab all the other mountain-climbing gear you need.

"Let's head for the roof," you tell Julie.

"Why don't we just go right out the window?" Julie demands. The rumbling of the building grows louder. "Come on! This place is going to crash down around us any second!"

"It's much safer if we go to the roof. We can anchor the rope to more stable things," you protest.

"I'm going out the window now," Julie declares. "If we go back into the stairwell, the vampire guard might get us. Besides, it'll take too long. Are you coming with me or not?"

Are you?

To stick to your plan and go up to the roof, turn to PAGE 108.

To rappel out the window with Julie right now, turn to PAGE 92.

You and Julie stand in the elevator studying Reggie's list.

Floor Seven: Final Showdown.

"It's time!" you declare, pointing to the words.

"Are you sure?" Julie asks.

"Yes!" you answer. "Do you have all the stuff we collected?"

"Yup, it's right here." Julie shifts the duffel bag to her other shoulder and pats the top.

"Ready?" you ask.

Julie nods slowly. You nod back.

You hope Julie doesn't notice your shaking hand as you push the Floor Seven button.

"This is it. The final showdown!" you announce as the elevator chugs into action.

Take a deep breath and turn to PAGE 58.

You yank your hand away from the furry surface.

"I found a light switch!" Julie yells from a distant corner. The overhead lights flash on.

Your mouth drops open. You're too terrified to scream.

You're face-to-face — well, face-to-chest — with a giant ape.

You must have been rubbing its chest!

"Wh-wha?" you stammer, stumbling away. What is an ape doing in Mayfield's Bazaar? What kind of crazy place is this?

A cursed department store, that's what, you remind yourself.

The ape's thick black fur gleams in the light. Huge muscles ripple as it moves toward you.

"*GRRRRR.*" A growl rumbles in the ape's throat. It rubs its broad chest slowly and gazes down at you, grunting and snorting.

You back up another step. You can't tell if it is friendly. And until you find out, you're not about to make any sudden moves.

But the ape likes sudden moves. Making them, that is.

With a fast, graceful leap, it jumps forward and grabs you!

Turn to PAGE 126.

"The volcano steam!" you whisper. "It gives off light."

Julie pulls the jar out of the duffel bag. It casts an eerie white glow over the floor.

There, not five feet away from you, stands a giant figure.

A monster-boy!

A colossal, hulking boy with thick muscles and strange orange skin. His head nearly scrapes the ceiling. Two twisted hands hang at his sides.

His huge eyes fix on you and Julie. The dim light of the volcano steam casts flickering shadows on his face, but you can make out his features. He looks like . . .

"*Reggie?*" you gasp.

"How are you doing with our bet?" the mutant roars. He picks up a display case filled with china dishes. He hurls it out of his way as if it were an empty pizza box!

And takes a step toward you.

Dash to PAGE 130.

"We'll take the test," you declare with confidence.

"And we'll pass it!" Julie joins in.

"Hooray!" all the gargoyles cheer. They jump up and down hooting and hollering in celebration. You can't help chuckling as you watch them — they're so goofy-looking.

But as you climb over the edge of the building onto the ledge, you stop feeling amused. Below you the streetlights glitter like jewels. The cold wind whips against you this high up.

You gulp. Your body shakes with fear. You inch along the ledge. Your back is pressed up to the coarse bricks of the building.

A beady-eyed pigeon blocks your path. You almost say, "Shoo!" but remember that part of the test is not making any sound. You kick at the pigeon. It pecks your ankle. Ow!

It startles you! You lean forward. . . .

And fall off the ledge! Into the air!

Speed to PAGE 49.

What is that thing? It's the size of a large dog, but its coat is a strange, shaggy gray color you've never seen on a dog.

The animal stands on its hind legs, like a bear. It moves into the pale light cast by the full moon through the windows.

The long, daggerlike claws on its front legs rip the air. The creature bares a set of sharp yellow fangs.

Dogs don't stand on their hind legs for so long. Even wolves and wild dogs can't do that.

Then the creature throws back its head and lets out a long, mournful howl.

You freeze in terror as you realize what the beast is.

"A werewolf!" you gasp.

Race to PAGE 90.

"I see the stairs!" Julie yells, pointing toward a flickering EXIT sign.

It's all the way across the women's clothing department. You're not sure you can make it over the heaving, shaking floorboards.

"What should we do?" you cry. "I don't know if we can get over there!"

"We could try to climb down the elevator shaft," Julie suggests frantically. "I think there's supposed to be a ladder inside in case you get stuck."

That's not a bad idea . . . although the stairs might be safer. But only if you can get to them.

Hurry, decide which way to go!

To climb down the ladder in the elevator shaft, turn to PAGE 111.

To cross the floor and take the stairs, turn to PAGE 45.

You feel your way along the wall. The flowery smell gets thicker . . . and thicker . . . and thicker. You fall to your knees, drowsy with the sweet scent.

Just before you shut your eyes and drift off, a hand grabs your arm.

You glance up and see a pair of brown eyes. It's Julie! She has tied her scarf over her nose. She looks like a bandit.

But the smell isn't getting to her. She drags you toward the elevator. You fall through the doors and collapse onto the elevator floor.

"Are you okay?" Julie asks, yanking off the scarf. The doors slide closed, muffling the sound of exploding bottles.

"Yeah, I'm okay," you reply. You sneeze three times and then take a deep breath. "And I managed to hold on to the Poisonous Perfume." You pull the bottle out of your pocket. You aren't sure why, but it didn't explode. Luckily!

"Great!" Julie exclaims. She stashes the bottle in the duffel bag. "Now let's go to another floor!"

Go to PAGE 99 and pick a new floor.

You swoosh down the rope, headed for the ground. Julie clambers along above you. It's going to feel so good to get away from Mayfield's!

Heavy claws suddenly rip into your jacket! You are yanked off the rope and into the air. Your harness snaps.

OH, NO! THE GARGOYLES CAN FLY! you realize.

The gargoyles carry you and Julie all night long. When dawn breaks, you seem to be in another part of the world altogether. You've never seen a city like this before. Crooked, plump buildings cluster together along twisting stone streets.

With a shock, you realize that all the people strolling in the street are gargoyles!

You're in a gargoyle city!

Turn to PAGE 133.

"No! Wrong!" Reggie's voice booms from the intercom. "There were only six volcanoes! You got it wrong!"

"I guess I didn't count right," you tell Reggie.

"You'll have to go up to the sixth floor now." Reggie sighs. "I tried to help you. But you'll have to face the volcano after all."

The intercom clicks off. The elevator jerks into motion and takes you up to Floor Six.

"What do you think Reggie meant about trying to help us?" you whisper to Julie. You have the creepy feeling he's still watching and listening.

"He was probably just trying to scare us," Julie replies.

The elevator opens onto Floor Six. A blast of hot air hits your face.

"Awesome!" you cry.

"Whoa!" Julie breathes. "Mine didn't look like *that*."

You both stare at a huge volcano in the middle of the floor.

Exploding jets of lava start to slurp over the side. The burning lava carries streams of fire across the floor.

Oh, no! The lava is headed straight for the elevator!

Race to PAGE 34.

86

"Niiiight!" Reggie's last word echoes in the small elevator. You're trapped — unless you do his puzzle.

"I guess we don't have much of a choice," Julie murmurs.

You reach down and find that one of the carpet's corners is loose. Sure enough, there's a note underneath it.

"Reggie did a lot of planning for this bet," you remark to Julie as you unfold the note.

The note reads:

Solve this word find! How many times can you find the word "VOLCANO"? The words can go forwards, backwards, up, down, and diagonally.

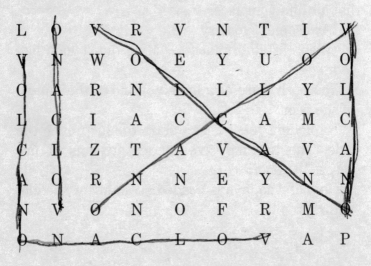

With a pencil, circle every VOLCANO. When you're done, count 'em up and turn to PAGE 70.

You and Julie shove through the door and dart down the stairs. You try to pull open the door on the next floor down.

Locked!

"Keep going," you pant. You dash down another flight. This time, the door opens.

"Quick, in here," you tell Julie. You're in the sporting goods department. You race past balls, bicycles, and Frisbees. You hear the vampire's feet clomping down the stairs.

"Hide!" you command. You've reached the teen department. You throw yourself into a huge bin holding thousands of pairs of socks. Julie hides in a clothing rack next to you.

You peek out of the bin. You watch, terrified, as the vampire night guard and his werewolf security dog burst through the door onto the fifth floor. The guard shines his flashlight back and forth, searching for you.

You scan the area frantically. There's a huge hole in the floor a few feet away. Damage caused by the earthquake, you figure. Maybe you could trick the guard and his dog into falling into the hole.

Or maybe you're better off staying put. The bin is a good hiding place.

To trick them into falling into the hole, turn to PAGE 59.

To keep hiding in the bin, turn to PAGE 61.

The scientist lunges for you. But you're too quick for her. You easily duck out of her reach. You scan the room. A door!

"Come on, Julie!" you shout. You and Julie dart toward the big metal door. Your fingers stretch for the doorknob.

KA-THUNK!

A thick iron bolt falls into place. It fastens itself over the latch.

You whirl around. Dr. Mayfield stands grinning beside the control panels. "The room is completely controlled from this console," she boasts.

She presses several more buttons. "Now there is no way for you to get away. Not with my army of mech-animals!"

CLINK! CLANK! The mutant half-toys, half-animals creak to life.

Turn to PAGE 43.

"Dummies coming to life," you gasp, wiping the sweat off your forehead. "The stories about this place are true!"

Julie shudders. "That was too weird."

You nod. What's waiting for us on the other floors? you wonder.

Julie must be worrying about the same thing. "Should we still try to win the bet?" she asks. "Or should we just get out of here?"

"I'm not sure," you reply. You think it over a moment.

Fighting the mannequins was frightening, but you escaped! You can still win. You just have to stay in the store for — you glance at Julie's Splotch watch — another fifty minutes.

"I want my prize," you declare. "Let's win the bet."

"Excellent!" Julie cries. She kneels on the floor and opens the new duffel bag. She shoves the leg inside.

"Which floor should we try next?" you ask Julie.

"We don't have to go in any special order," Julie reminds you. "But we have to go to *all* of them. Let's look at Reggie's note again."

Turn to PAGE 99 to see Reggie's note with the master list of floors.

The ferocious beast hears you. Its head whips around, and it snarls at you and Julie. You see that instead of eyes, the beast has two red flames!

The earthquake ... the red-eyed monsters ...

The stories are true. This department store is cursed!

A plank tumbles down from the ceiling and crashes at your feet. You snatch it up, gripping it like a baseball bat. If the werewolf attacks, you're ready for it.

Sort of.

You stare at the terrifying half-human and half-animal creature.

"What do we do?" Julie whispers, her voice hoarse with fear. "Should we try to run past the werewolf or fight it?"

"If we get by it, maybe we can lock the stair door from the other side," you reason. "But it might catch us as we run past. Maybe we should just try to fight it." You grip the plank tighter.

The werewolf growls and licks its chops.

To race past the werewolf and try to lock the door, turn to PAGE 69.

To fight the werewolf with the stick, turn to PAGE 105.

"You found the Poisonous Perfume. Excellent!" Julie congratulates you.

You grab the bottle and slip it into your pocket.

BAM! One of the bottles on the table explodes. Glass and perfume spray you and Julie.

"Whoa!" you cry, backing up. "Why did that bottle explode?"

POP! Another one blows up.

"There must be something wrong with them," Julie declares, covering her head with her hands.

POP! BOOM! More bottles burst open. Tiny slivers of glass fly everywhere.

"What's happening?" you exclaim. "Do you think taking the Poisonous Perfume caused this?"

"Let's not try to figure it out now," Julie cries. "Let's just get out of here!"

You turn to follow Julie, when a huge display bottle explodes. It sprays you right in the face.

"Aaaaaaggghhh!" you wail. "The perfume is blinding me."

You blink rapidly. Your eyes water like crazy. You gasp for breath, but the perfume-filled air is choking you.

"Hurry!" you hear Julie shout.

But you can't even see where she is!

Flip to PAGE 11 before you choke!

The building shakes again. Hard.

"You're right," you tell Julie. "Why waste any more time? We should rappel out the window."

"Now you're talking!" Julie replies with a smile. "Show me how to hook up this gear."

You help Julie put on her body harness. You hook the rope up to a solid-looking marble pillar.

"Just push off from the wall with your feet and swoop down," you instruct your friend.

Julie holds the rope and slips out the window. You hang out the window, watching her progress. When Julie is halfway down, you join her on the rope.

You rappel down. Five feet — ten feet — twenty feet. You feel as if you're flying through the crisp night air.

You feel a tweak on the rope. You glance up. At the window above, you spot two sinister red flames. The red-eyed vampire!

You watch in horror as the creature flashes his fangs . . . and uses them to slice your rope.

Too bad you let Julie rope you into rappelling out the window. Well, you wanted a quick way down. And you got it. It's called gravity!

THE END

"Who's there?" you call into the darkness.

"Don't you recognize my voice?" the creepy voice asks.

It sounds like . . . could it be . . . ?

"*Reggie?*" you ask.

"Yup," his voice replies. "I've been watching your progress on the security monitors."

"You've been spying on us?" Julie demands.

"It's been a riot." Reggie's laugh comes through the intercom in the elevator. "Ready to quit?"

"No way," you snap. "Start this elevator back up! We're going to the sixth floor. You're slowing us down."

"I'll make you a deal. I'll *give* you the volcano steam if you can figure out a little puzzle of mine!"

"What are you talking about, Reggie?" you challenge him.

"Look under the carpet." The lights in the elevator flash back on. "You'll find a puzzle I left for you."

"Maybe we don't want to do your stupid puzzle," you retort.

"Yeah," Julie chimes in. "And besides, I want to see the volcano model on Floor Six!"

"You don't *have* to do my puzzle," Reggie says. "You can just sit in the elevator . . . all night!"

You know what you have to do. Turn to PAGE 86.

Your heart clutches as you fall forward into the elevator shaft.

A hand grabs your arm firmly. "Gotcha!" Julie cries triumphantly. She steadies you and hauls you away from the edge of the elevator shaft.

"You saved my life!" you gasp. "Thanks!"

CRRREEEAAAKKKK!

The building shudders, trembling harder and harder. Glass counters crash to the ground.

"Quick, we've got to get out of here!" Julie shouts.

You peer into the elevator shaft again. This time you have a good hold on the elevator doorway so you won't fall.

You spot a narrow metal ladder on the wall. The trouble is, it looks black with grease. It might be slippery.

You also notice a heavy steel cable attached to a pulley. You might be able to slide down the cable. It would be a lot faster than climbing down — but maybe more dangerous.

CRASH! A set of tall shelves topples inches away from you.

Fast seems important!

To climb down the ladder, turn to PAGE 7.
To slide down the cable, turn to PAGE 102.

You can't believe it! The mannequin has come to life!

"Give me back my leg, now!" the dummy roars. It sneers.

Your heart races with fear. Reggie's stories are true! The store is cursed!

The plastic man grips your arm tightly. But you don't let go of the leg in your other hand. "Julie!" you yell. "Catch!" You toss the leg to Julie.

"Give it *back*!" the mannequin shouts.

Julie's scream startles you. "Oh, no!" she cries. "They're all coming to life! What do we do?"

She's right! Mannequins all around the floor are stretching, as if waking up from a long nap.

You yank your arm out of the mannequin's tight grasp. He falls over, crashing to the ground.

"Help!" the mannequin in the tuxedo yells. "These punks took my leg!"

Slowly, all the mannequins' heads turn toward you and Julie.

"Get them!" the fallen one commands.

With jerky robotic movements, the big plastic mannequins step off their platforms. They lurch toward you and Julie!

Turn to PAGE 53, quick!

Julie leans over and examines your cardboard arm. Then she peers at the glitter-covered baby.

"I think that glitter made you flat," she murmurs. "How can I get it off?"

She glances around and sees the hardware department on the other side of the floor.

"I could get a fan and blow the glitter off," she tells you. Then she looks toward the rest rooms. "Or I could try to wipe it off with a wet paper towel."

"Which do you want me to try?" Julie asks you. "I'll say 'fan' or 'paper towel' and you nod for the one you want."

To use a wet paper towel, turn to PAGE 64.
To use the wind from a fan, turn to PAGE 109.

"It's almost one," you assure Julie. "We can last till then."

Or not.

"Found you!" Reggie hovers over you and Julie. He opens his mouth wide. His big green teeth come closer and closer.

"Wait!" you scream. "Don't eat us. We taste terrible!"

"Yeah," Julie adds. "And our hands are stuck in this stupid backpack. You'll have to eat that too."

Reggie's huge eyes narrow. He seems to be thinking it over.

You raise the Heart Attack Backpack high in the air. So high, Julie is forced onto her tiptoes. You shake it at Reggie.

"It's made out of nylon!" you inform him. "It's not edible."

Julie nods. "And you'd have to swallow us both together. You might choke."

"Who cares?" Reggie bellows. "I'm hungry!" He smacks his giant lips.

Your knees buckle in fear. You and Julie fall to the ground.

Turn to PAGE 10.

Gargoyles creep toward you from every direction. They form a ring around you and Julie. There are a dozen of them. In the moonlight you can see their skin is rubbery. The mottled gray color looks almost exactly like stone.

All of the gargoyles are grinning at you. You can't tell if they're friendly or if there is something sinister in their smiles.

Your mind races. Maybe Julie could distract the gargoyles while you hook up the mountain-climbing gear. Then you could both jump over the side of the building and rappel to safety.

Or maybe you should just reason with them. They might even be helpful. After all, they are smiling. . . .

One of the gargoyles lurches forward. It wears a stone crown set at a jaunty angle. On its back are large, bony bat wings. Its claws clatter on the roof's surface.

Make up your mind. What's the best way to handle these strange creatures?

To ask *Julie* to distract them while you set up the gear, turn to PAGE 25.

To try talking to the gargoyles, turn to PAGE 131.

You pull the note out of your jean jacket and unfold it.

To prove that you explored the whole store, it says that you have to bring Reggie one thing from each floor.

Floor 1: A Man's Leg

Floor 2: Poisonous Perfume

Floor 3: Heart Attack Backpack

Floor 4: Baby Booties

Floor 5: Silver Arrow

Floor 6: Volcano Steam

Floor 7: Final Showdown

Pick a floor, any floor. Remember, you don't have to go in any particular order. To go to:

Floor Two, turn to PAGE 22
Floor Three, turn to PAGE 33
Floor Four, turn to PAGE 44
Floor Five, turn to PAGE 55
Floor Six, turn to PAGE 66
When you are ready for the Final Showdown, turn to PAGE 77.

"Get out the perfume!" you tell Julie. "I'm going to spray it right in Reggie's face!"

Julie pulls out the bottle of perfume. She hands it to you.

The huge, mutant Reggie lets out a roar.

"I'M HUNGRY!" he bellows.

"Quick! Spray him! Spray him!" Julie yells.

Did you do the maze and find the REAL poisonous perfume? Or did you grab any old bottle and use up most of it on the termites?

Turn to PAGE 63 if you have the real stuff.

If you just have any old perfume, FORGET IT! Use the backpack on PAGE 37.

"Come over here, kids," the judge instructs you.

You and Julie stroll over to the judge's stand. You wonder what kind of present the mannequins will give you. It could be something great — they have the whole store to choose from!

You and Julie wait in front of the judge. A mannequin flanks each of you. They lay their hands on your shoulders. The judge reaches out and places a hand on your head.

VRRROOOOOSSHH! A surge of energy jolts through you. Your entire body stiffens. But once the strange current subsides, your body doesn't return to normal. Instead, you feel as if you are frozen solid.

You try to scream, but your mouth doesn't open! You try to turn to see Julie, but your neck won't move! What happened?

What's the matter — don't you like your gift?

You see, the mannequins felt so awful about mistreating you that they wanted to give you something really special. The best present they could think of.

That's right. Life as a mannequin.

Now isn't that nice?

THE END

102

"Let's slide down that cable," you suggest. "It would be quickest. And I'm sure it's strong enough to hold us."

"Great idea. But wait." Julie grabs two pairs of heavy leather gloves from a nearby display. "Put these on. You'll be able to hold on better."

You pull the gloves on and grab the cable. It's sticky.

"Here goes nothing!" You lean forward and swing into the shaft. You grip the cable tightly, trying to control your speed. You inch down.

Around you, the building shakes and heaves, but the cable is surprisingly still. You're making good progress.

You glance up. The rectangle of light from the seventh floor is getting smaller. Julie clings to the cable above you.

Your arms are getting tired. You wonder if maybe this wasn't such a good idea.

Slide down to PAGE 31.

You've picked up every bottle on the table, and you still haven't found the Poisonous Perfume. Where *is* it?

"We have to hurry," Julie coaxes you. "Just take any old bottle!"

"But it might be important later," you protest.

"But it might not be important at all," Julie points out.

You happen to glance at a huge display cabinet across the aisle. Your heart sinks. Hundreds of perfume bottles — that you haven't looked through yet — line its shelves.

Julie's right. You've already spent too much time on this floor.

Give in on PAGE 26.

Your whole body is prickling. You collapse to the soft carpet. Now you feel as if you're being crushed by a steamroller!

"You're flat!" Julie shrieks. "You're as flat as a pancake! You're . . . *cardboard!*"

You try to groan. Every muscle hurts. No sound comes out. You lift up your hand and stare in horror. It's flat.

If you didn't know before, you do now. This *is* a cursed store.

And you are its victim. Somehow you turned to cardboard, just by touching that baby figure.

You remember the glitter on the baby. Maybe it was magic!

Julie covers her eyes. "I can't look," she groans. "Tell me this isn't happening!"

You gaze helplessly up from the floor at Julie.

Then your new cardboard eyes widen in terror. You wave your flat arms, trying to signal Julie. But it's no use.

Her eyes are still covered. She doesn't see the mother and father cardboard figures creeping up behind her.

Flip to PAGE 35.

"We should take care of this monster now!" you urge Julie. Julie finds another plank in the rubble and arms herself.

You notice the building isn't trembling so violently anymore. The rumbling lessens, and the shaking slows down. Finally, it stops completely.

"I guess the earthquake is over," Julie murmurs.

"For now," you comment. Both of you focus on the werewolf. It drops back down to all fours again. The bristly fur on its back stands straight up. It growls at you.

You take a deep breath and clutch the plank tightly. You prepare to fight.

A beam of light shines around the corner. A flashlight! Maybe it's some kind of rescue squad, you think. Your heart pounds hard in your chest. Hope surges in you.

"Over here!" you call. "Help us! We're over here!"

The fire-eyed werewolf lets out another long howl.

Try to stay calm and turn to PAGE 28.

106

"Let me go, you big creep!" Julie struggles in Reggie's tight grip. But he's too strong for her.

You have one last hope — the magic scroll the archer gave you.

He said you would need magic for the final challenge. You hope it works now!

You dig frantically through the duffel bag. Finally, your hand brushes the scroll. You grab it and rip off the fancy scarlet ribbon.

"'Onwe huppak minodot!'" you read from the cracked parchment. "'Burnah bunrat Rumina-cha-cha!'"

Reggie freezes. He glances at you with a puzzled expression. It turns to fury.

"Noooooo!" he roars at you in anger.

Quick! Race to PAGE 62.

"Let's try to make peace with him," you tell Julie. "The basketball idea is too risky." Your stomach feels as if it's twisted in knots. "Do you have anything white we can wave?"

"Yeah," Julie replies. She pulls a used, crumpled-up tissue out of her pocket. "Wave this."

"Gross!" You grasp the dirty tissue with the tips of your fingers and wave it above your head.

The stream of arrows stops immediately.

"We surrender!" Julie shouts.

"Yeah! We give up," you call. "Please don't shoot us!"

"Present yourselves," the archer shouts.

You and Julie scuttle out from behind the stack of basketballs. Half the balls are deflated. There are so many arrows sticking out of them, the display looks like a giant, orange porcupine.

The archer strides up to you and Julie.

"Young roustabouts!" he barks. "Why have you entered my domain?"

Well? He's waiting! Hurry up and explain on PAGE 48.

"Rappelling is risky as it is," you tell Julie. "If we rappel out of this window, we won't be anchored securely. Let's go up to the roof."

"I guess you're right," Julie replies with a shrug. "But let's hurry before the building collapses!"

You and Julie run to the stairway as fast as you can. Your arms are laden with the heavy mountain-climbing equipment. You glance to the floor below. The vampire still lies there, motionless. You hope he stays that way!

You climb the stairs to the top floor and then up one more flight of stairs, to the roof.

A big white sign declares: NO ADMITTANCE. Another says: EMERGENCY EXIT ONLY.

"I'd say this is an emergency, wouldn't you?" you shout to Julie. The building heaves under your feet.

"Definitely," Julie agrees. She pushes open the door.

The full moon lights up the roof. Gray, silver-edged clouds creep across the dark sky.

Julie grabs your arms. Hard. Her eyes are wide with fear as she points at something.

"M-m-m-monster!"

Turn to PAGE 38. Fast!

"Should I try the fan?" Julie questions.

You nod.

"I hope this works," she says as she walks off. "No offense, but as a poster child, you give me the creeps."

Julie returns with a fan a minute later. She flips it on.

Please let this work, you think.

The wind from the fan blows on you. Then it blows you into the air.

You're flying! Toward the ceiling.

Toward a giant, rotating ceiling fan.

With sharp metal blades!

Flutter to PAGE 56.

The magic scroll! This must be the time to use it! The archer said you would need it to fight the fierce beast on Floor Seven.

With a grunt, the ape tosses you in the air and catches you.

"Julie!" you cry. "Use the magic scroll! Read the charm!"

"Good idea!" Julie drops the big black duffel bag to the ground and rummages through it.

"It says that this charm will turn any monster into a regular kid. It's perfect!" Julie tells you.

The ape must be bored with tossing you up in the air. It starts a new game — shaking you around. The ape shakes you so hard, your sneaker flies off. It sails through the air and hits Julie.

"Oh, no! It ripped the scroll!" She holds up two jagged pieces of parchment. "I don't know which half goes first," she moans.

Turn to PAGE 128.

"We'll never reach the stairs!" you yell over the crashing sounds of the building falling apart. "Let's climb down the elevator shaft."

"Help me pull open the doors," Julie orders. Together you manage to pry them open.

You peer down the shaft. Thick black grease coats the cables and machinery. You can see all the way down to the crashed elevator car at the bottom of the shaft.

The building shakes harder. You lose your balance and pitch forward!

You throw your arms out, trying to catch the elevator door . . . a cable . . . anything. . . .

But it's no good.

You're falling into the black elevator shaft.

Drop to PAGE 94.

"Let's take the steps," you decide. "We need to put as much distance between us and that vampire as possible!"

"Okay," Julie agrees. "But be careful."

You start down the stairs. Julie follows cautiously behind. So far, so good.

"You'll never get away from me!"

Oh, no! The vampire looms over you at the top of the stairs.

"Hurry!" you cry. You pick up speed, rushing down the steps.

WHAM! The slick oil makes your feet fly out from under you. Total wipeout.

"Yikes!" Julie shrieks. She tumbles over you.

The vampire's cruel laughter echoes in the stairwell.

You try to pull yourself up. But every attempt to stand sends you sprawling. Julie doesn't do any better.

But the vampire has no trouble at all. He just turns into a bat! He easily flies down — and bites you.

So that's it. You and Julie aren't kids anymore. You're horrible vampires.

All because of your decision to try the stairs, despite the slippery oil.

"FANGS," Julie mutters sarcastically. "FANGS a lot!"

THE END

THUMP! You land on a huge pile of baby sweaters.

"That was close," Julie declares, jogging over.

"That was *really* close," you agree.

"That was *too* close!" Julie adds.

"I thought I was going to be shredded by that ceiling fan!" you say, wiping beads of sweat off your face.

"And you almost landed on that glass display case full of silver rattles," Julie points out.

"Let's leave this floor, okay?" you moan.

"You got it!" Julie lays a hand on your shoulder.

You spot something on the ground. A little cellophane-wrapped package of baby booties!

"Hey," you cry. "Look what I found!"

You hand them to Julie. She puts the booties in the duffel bag. And you both step into the elevator. Time to choose another floor.

Go to PAGE 99 and pick again.

As Reggie lurches toward you, your fingers grasp the baby booties. You yank them from the bag. The tiny socks are tied together by a long piece of yarn. Just long enough to trip the mutant . . . you hope.

You toss one of the booties to Julie. Reggie lunges forward.

"Pull!" you shout. Reggie stumbles over the yarn.

SNAP! The yarn breaks! Just like that!

But it did its job, because Reggie is falling.

He's falling . . . right on top of you!

Tripping Reggie was a good idea.

But you should have made sure he wouldn't fall on you!

SPLAT!

Gross! Just be glad you don't have to clean up the mess. Squished kids are almost impossible to get out of a carpet.

THE END

With a burst of energy, you lift yourself from the floor and hurtle toward the trap. You soar over the gaping hole hidden under the coats.

You make it!

Just as you hoped, the werewolf runs across the coats. *WHOOSH!* It falls through the hole.

WHAM! You hear it land on the floor below. It lets out a pathetic whimper. The vampire races up to the hole and gazes down at his pet.

"You kids will pay!" the vampire murmurs, baring his fangs. He steps around the hole and stalks toward you and Julie. His pale hands stretch toward you. His red eyes flare in anger.

"You will pay for hurting my little puppy!" He draws closer.

"Run!" Julie screams.

To the right of the guard is a big pile of clothes. It might be too high to jump over. But to the left of the vampire is a mannequin. It could block your way.

Do you run around the guard to the left or the right?

To run to the right, turn to PAGE 124.
To run to the left, turn to PAGE 65.

"GIVE US THE LEG!" the mannequins moan.

"You want it — you got it!" you scream.

With all your strength, you hurl the leg at the attacking. mannequins. Three of them between you and the elevator topple over like bowling pins.

"Way to go!" Julie cheers.

It's the break you need.

"Come on, Julie!" you yell, racing into the elevator.

She jumps in behind you and jabs at the Door Close button.

The mannequins are crawling over each other to get to you.

"Close, doors, close!" Julie pleads, pounding the button.

A big mannequin in a jogger's outfit reaches the elevator just as the doors glide closed. He jams his leg into the narrowing gap.

"No!" Julie gasps.

But the doors are powerful. With a crunching *SNAP*, the leg comes off!

The doors close.

"We made it!" you exclaim.

"And we got our leg," Julie adds, picking up the mangled mannequin limb.

Hop to PAGE 89.

You and Julie cover your ears as Reggie yells over the elevator intercom, "NOOOO!"

Your brows furrow. "Did I get it wrong?" you ask.

"No! You got it right! You got all six of them! I spent a long time on that puzzle," Reggie whines. "I can't believe you got it right."

"Yes!" you exclaim. Julie gives you a high five.

"You won the volcano steam fair and square," Reggie grumbles.

You jump when something prods you in the back. You turn and discover that a small drawer has slid out of the elevator wall.

There, in the red velvet-lined drawer, sits a glass jar. Inside floats a tiny white cloud. Light shines from the bottle. It's so bright, you can hardly make out the label. It reads: VOLCANO STEAM.

"Cool! We got the steam!" Julie slips the glowing jar into the duffel bag. "And we didn't even have to go to the sixth floor! We'll make our one-hour deadline for sure!"

Good work! Now go to PAGE 99 to choose another floor.

"Did you say the ladder stops?" you repeat. You can barely hear her over the quaking of the building.

"Yes," she yells up to you. "Now what do we do?"

A tiny whirring sound catches your attention. Climbing down a pulley near you is a small mechanical monkey wearing a red velvet vest!

You draw in your breath with a surprised gasp.

"You're never going to believe this . . . ," you call to Julie. "But look!"

Julie glances up the ladder at you. "Is that a toy monkey?" she cries.

The little monkey gazes at you with shining black eyes. Then, with jerky mechanical motions, it turns around. It starts moving away from you.

"Let's follow it!" you urge.

"Why?" Julie demands.

"Because it had to come from somewhere," you reply. "And it could lead to a way out."

"I guess you have a point," Julie mumbles. "Okay, let's go."

Follow the monkey to PAGE 23.

You wrap your fingers around the fire alarm's lever. And yank it as hard as you can.

Immediately, sirens wail and bright red strobe lights flash. A shower of water rains down on you and Julie. The cloud of perfume disintegrates. The bottles stop exploding.

"I'm so glad you pulled that alarm," Julie remarks. "That perfume was making me gag. And I was scared because I couldn't see where you were. I thought we were in trouble."

It's nice of Julie to say that. But you *are* in trouble.

Big trouble.

Because when the fire department breaks down the doors to Mayfield's Bazaar and finds you both standing in ten thousand dollars' worth of broken perfume bottles, the officers think your story smells fishy.

Exploding perfume bottles . . . yeah, right.

Your parents ground you — for a year!

Worst of all, no matter how hard you scrub, you can't get rid of the stench of all that perfume.

It *stinks*, but this is

THE END.

120

"Need — something — sharp!" you gasp to Julie. "To — cut — it — off!"

The backpack gives a hard squeeze. You're getting so dizzy that the room spins. Tiny dots appear in front of your eyes.

You and Julie dash behind counters and plow though drawers. The pressure from the backpack makes it almost impossible for you to keep going.

"Can't — find — anything!" You huff and puff.

"Me neither," Julie yells.

You can hardly breathe. You fall to your knees. Then to your side.

The backpack chokes you so hard, it feels as if your heart is pounding in your throat.

You need a lucky break. Fast!

If you've already visited Floor Five, turn to PAGE 40.

If you haven't been to Floor Five yet, turn to PAGE 12.

"I didn't *mean* to take the watch," Julie assures you. "So I don't think I'm guilty."

"You're right," you agree. "You made a mistake! We're kids — we're allowed to make mistakes!"

"Your honor," Julie addresses the judge. "We plead not guilty. By reason of forgetting the watch was still on my wrist."

The room falls silent.

The only sound is your heart pounding in your chest.

Will they believe you?

A juror mannequin rises stiffly to her feet. "We accept your plea." She smiles sympathetically at you. "I know just how it is," she adds. "I forget things myself all the time."

Other mannequins chime in. "Yeah, besides, they're just kids."

"She meant to return the watch."

"I believe them."

The judge leans over to speak to you. "We feel terrible about your rough treatment." He glares at the police mannequin. "To make up for it, we will give you a great gift."

You grin at Julie. This is turning out a whole lot better than you expected!

Turn to PAGE 101 for your special gift.

"It's from Reggie," you declare, plucking the note off the elevator wall. "It must have more instructions."

"'To prove that you explored the whole store, you have to bring me one thing from each floor,'" Julie reads over your shoulder. She picks up the duffel bag. "This must be to put all the stuff in."

"Cool," you exclaim. "This will be fun! Like a scavenger hunt."

"Yeah, but look what he wants us to get on Floor One!" Julie points at the notebook paper.

It says: A MAN'S LEG.

You swallow hard. "I don't like the way that sounds," you mutter.

"A man's leg? What does that mean?" Julie's forehead wrinkles.

You shove the note into the pocket of your denim jacket.

"There's only one way to find out," you say.

Then you press the button for the first floor.

Turn to PAGE 132.

"I've always wanted to try a time machine," you exclaim. "We'll give you the animals if you let us try it!"

"You've got yourself a deal," the old lady replies.

You place the metal kitten in her hands. Julie sets down the mechanical dog.

"The time machine is over there. Go climb in." Dr. Mayfield points at a big broken-down-looking metal box. You don't notice any buttons or knobs or wires. It resembles a big metal storage cabinet.

"Are you sure this is a good idea?" Julie whispers to you.

"Yeah! Come on, it'll be awesome. Time travel! We'll be famous. We can check out the cavemen!" You're already imagining all sorts of amazing adventures. You pull open the metal doors.

CREAK! You glance inside. Cobwebs linger in the corners. It looks as if it hasn't been used in a long time, but you climb inside anyway. Julie follows you, reluctantly.

SLAM! Dr. Mayfield shuts the doors behind you.

"Ha-ha-ha!" she cackles. "You fell for the oldest trick in the book! Time-travel in an old locker — I don't think so!"

If only you *could* travel back in time — to the beginning of this whole bet! But unfortunately, it's not the beginning. It's

THE END.

You dodge the vampire, dashing to his right. You bend your knees deeply and leap. Yes! You clear the pile of clothes. Ahead of you is the bright red light of an EXIT sign.

"This way, Julie," you shout. "I found the stairs!"

The red-eyed vampire night guard chases you. You hear him grunting with effort.

"I will have revenge for my puppy!" he hollers.

You push open the door to the stairs. Something is wrong. . . .

The stairs are covered in slimy black goop. It looks like oil. Slick, dangerous oil. Above your head you spot a broken pipe. That must be where the oil came from, you realize.

Julie bounds toward you. "Look out!" you cry.

"What is it?" Julie asks breathlessly, skidding to a stop.

"The stairs are covered with oil," you explain. "They might be too slippery to climb down."

"But this is the only way down," Julie says.

You rub your face, trying to think. "Or we could trip the vampire," you suggest. "He'd go flying down those stairs."

Julie eyes the stairs. "I don't know. . . ."

So it's up to you.

Do you want to try the stairs, anyway? Turn to PAGE 112.

Or do you want to trip the vampire guard? Turn to PAGE 13.

You decide to spray the termites with the perfume. Squishing them with your own body is too gross. Even for you.

You fumble with the perfume bottle. You pop off the cap just as a big, squiggling insect crawls up your nose.

"Yuck!" You shake your head violently. The termite plops onto the floor. You take aim.

SQUIRT! You spray perfume on the termites clinging to your body.

FIZZ! PFFFFTT! The alcohol in the spray shrivels them. They curl up into balls and fall to the ground.

You rush over to Julie and spray the ones clinging to her.

You and Julie dash to the elevator. Dozens of shriveled termite bodies make *POP!* sounds when you run over them.

"There's only a little perfume left," you gasp. "I hope we don't need it for anything else."

"I hope we don't run into anything else that bites!" Julie answers. "Where to next?"

Turn to PAGE 99 to pick another floor.

The giant ape clutches you to its chest. It stares you straight in the eye. You watch in horror as red flames swirl in its eyes.

This must be one of the red-eyed monsters Reggie is always talking about, you realize.

"Help!" you call to Julie. She rushes over as you struggle to get out of the ape's hairy arms.

The ape lifts you up in the air, then bounces you on the ground. It hoots and snorts. It bounces you again.

The giant ape thinks you're a toy!

"I don't think it's going to hurt you," Julie assures you.

"That's easy for you to say," you cry. The ape dangles you by the arms and then bounces you again.

The ape lifts you over its head. Oh, no! It's going to throw you like a ball!

You have to think fast. When you rubbed its chest, the ape seemed calm. You could try doing that again.

Or maybe one of the items you have in the duffel bag would distract the ape.

To try rubbing the ape's chest, turn to PAGE 5.
If you have the archer's magic scroll in the duffel bag, you could try that on PAGE 110.

The creatures make strange whirring and clicking sounds. Then they start going berserk! Yowling, yelping, clicking, clacking — the noise is deafening.

Mech-dogs chase the mech-cats around the room. "Stop!" You reach out to grab a yapping dog. "Yeow! It bit me!"

"It's the food," Dr. Mayfield snaps. "They were trained to respond only to my command. But now . . ."

The lights flicker on and off, and then with a loud *POP!* the room plunges into darkness.

"What happened?" Julie cries.

A tiny penlight flicks on by the console. "The animals have gnawed through the cables," Dr. Mayfield informs you. "Now we may never get out of here."

A mech-bird dives at you. "Aaah!" you shriek, throwing your hands up to protect your face.

Julie's wails and Dr. Mayfield's screams join yours in the darkness. But they're nearly drowned out by the calls and cries of the vicious, crazed beasts.

Shudder with terror and shut the book. Because this story has come to a beastly

END.

"Just read the charm!" you gasp. "Fast!"

The ape gives you an extra-hard squeeze. Lights flash in front of your eyes.

"Weeell, okay," Julie replies, looking at both pieces of paper. She holds one up.

"Malery Blalery Gwendoo Boo," she chants. "Alchel Alchel Marbados Goo . . . "

As Julie reads the charm, you feel a funny sensation all over your body. Your skin tingles. You glance down.

Hair is sprouting all over you! Your arms grow longer. The foot that's missing a sneaker bursts through its sock. Your other foot tears through the shoe. Your big toes look like thumbs.

The ape stares at you. Its red eyes widen in shock as it drops you.

Your long arms dangle. Your knuckles trail on the floor. You feel your lips swell into a muzzle. Your breath comes in snorts and grunts.

Julie must have read the second half of the spell first, you realize. Instead of turning the ape into a kid, it turned you into an ape!

You look at the other ape. It's staring at you lovingly! Now it's puckering its ape lips and reaching toward you. Looks like you won't be lonely, anyway.

THE END

"Help me!" Julie screams.

You stare at the mannequin's leg. The way Reggie is holding his arms up gives you an idea.

"Tickle, tickle, tickle . . . ," you tease. You use the mannequin's toes to tickle Reggie's armpit.

"Hee-hee. . . ." It works! "Hee-hee! Haw-haw-haw!" Reggie lowers Julie gently. Soon he's rolling on the ground like a big puppy.

"Let's sneak away," Julie whispers.

You set down the leg and tiptoe away. But as soon as you reach the door, Reggie roars with anger.

"MORE TICKLING!" he demands.

In fact, every time you try to leave, Reggie gets really mad. You have to stay and tickle him until one A.M. when he turns normal again.

It's not so bad. But you *are* late getting home.

Which means when your parents come home, say good night to the baby-sitter, and go up to check on you, they discover you sneaked out. Busted!

You might be able to escape from a cursed department store, but you can't escape being punished!

In fact, you end up with the Rollerblades you wanted — but by the time your mother lets you go blading, they don't fit anymore!

THE END

130

"Reggie? Is that really you?" you ask. You and Julie back away from the hulking giant.

"Yeah, it's me. Part of the curse of Mayfield's is that at midnight I turn into a mutant. It only lasts for an hour, but it's a long hour. And I get really hungry. That's why I made this bet with you guys."

He cracks his huge knuckles — they're the size of onions.

A jolt of fear zips through your system.

"We've got to fight him!" you whisper to Julie. "He wants to EAT us!"

You and Julie dash behind a counter.

But Reggie towers high above you. He can easily spot your hiding place. His giant feet crunch over broken glass on the carpet. Drool trails from his mouth.

"We have all that stuff we collected," Julie murmurs to you. "Maybe we can fight him with something from the bag."

You think about some of the stuff you could use. . . .

If you have the Poisonous Perfume, you can spray Reggie in the face with it on PAGE 100.

If you have the Heart Attack Backpack, you can throw it at him on PAGE 37.

The gargoyles crouch all around you. The guy with the crown seems to be their leader. He scuttles closer to you and Julie.

They're cute, you think. In an ugly sort of way.

"Hello." You smile nervously at the gargoyle. "Nice to meet you."

"Hiya," the gargoyle replies. His voice sounds more like a belch. He scratches his belly and adjusts his crown. "How ya doin'? My name's Craig T. Kelly."

You can't believe it! He's friendly *and* he speaks English!

"We're okay, Mr. Kelly," you answer politely. "But we're in a hurry to get off this building before it crashes to the ground."

The gargoyle chuckles. "Don't sweat it," he hoots. "This building shakes every night."

"But it makes us really nervous," Julie says.

"Could you help us find a safe way down?" you ask.

"That depends." The gargoyle's face grows serious.

"On what?" Julie blurts out.

"On whether you stand up to THE TEST," the gargoyle growls.

Turn to PAGE 47.

The elevator glides upward. The doors open onto Floor One. You and Julie step out into the dimly lit men's clothing department. A dozen mannequins stand on a nearby platform, modeling blazers, sweaters, and suits.

"Where are we supposed to get a man's leg?" Julie wonders aloud.

"Let's take a leg from one of these mannequins," you declare. "They're men. Sort of."

Julie grins. "Perfect! I bet that's just what Reggie had in mind."

"Excuse me, sir," you joke, strolling over to a mannequin in a black tuxedo. "I need to borrow your leg."

As Julie laughs, you hear a deep, bonging sound. It's a grandfather clock, striking twelve.

It's the time when the store is supposed to go crazy! You and Julie give each other a long look.

Then you crouch beside the mannequin. You twist its left leg out of the plastic socket and slide it from the tuxedo trousers.

A cold, strong hand suddenly grabs your arm.

The hand is smooth and shiny. You glance up in shock.

It's the mannequin! Its face peers at you coldly.

"Give me back my leg!" the plastic dummy moans.

Hurry to PAGE 95.

The gargoyles fly you and Julie to the top of a big department store. You notice other kids scattered along the roof, the ledges, and windowsills.

You have a funny feeling the favorite decorating style in the gargoyle city involves humans.

The gargoyle sets you down on a narrow ledge. It forces you to crouch down and bare your teeth.

"Now sit very still," it orders you. "FOREVER!"

THE END

About R.L. Stine

R.L. Stine is the most popular author in America. He is the creator of the *Goosebumps*, *Give Yourself Goosebumps*, *Fear Street*, and *Ghosts of Fear Street* series, among other popular books. He has written more than 100 scary novels for kids. Bob lives in New York City with his wife, Jane, teenage son, Matt, and dog, Nadine.

SHE'S NOT A TOY.
SHE'S NOT YOUR FRIEND.
SHE'S AN EVIL DOLL
AND SHE'S ALIVE.

Goosebumps®
SERIES 2000
R.L. STINE

Book #2: Bride of the Living Dummy

The next millennium will shock you.
In bookstores this February.

◣ SCHOLASTIC    PARACHUTE

Don't let any Goosebumps® books CREEP past you!

$3.99 EACH

Scare me, thrill me, mail me GOOSEBUMPS now!

Available wherever you buy books, or use this order form.
Scholastic Inc., P.O. Box 7502, Jefferson City, MO 65102

Please send me the books I have checked above. I am enclosing $_____ (please add $2.00 to cover shipping and handling). Send check or money order—no cash or C.O.D.s please.

Name _____ Age_____

Address _____

City _____ State/Zip _____

Please allow four to six weeks for delivery. Offer good in the U.S. only. Sorry, mail orders are not available to residents of Canada. Prices subject to change.

We Interrupt This Book to Bring You an Important Announcement!

GIVE YOURSELF

The First Special Edition!

Goosebumps®

R.L. STINE

Even More Dangerous Surprises!

The Ultimate Challenge

You're on a class field trip to the Hall of Science, when a strange computer message warns you: "The Super Computer Has Taken Over." Now you're trapped—and you'll need help to find a safe way out. Pick up objects to help you. Roll the dice to find your fate. Watch out for the vats of acid and the moving dinosaur skeletons. And whatever you do... Never, NEVER give up....

Only One Way Out!

Give Yourself Goosebumps Special Edition #1
Into the Jaws of Doom

In Your Bookstore This January